Ghosthunters

and the

Muddy

Monster

of

Doom!

Ghosthunters

and the

Muddy

Monster

of

Doom!

by CORNELIA FUNKE

Chicken House

SCHOLASTIC INC.

New York   Toronto   London   Auckland   Sydney
Mexico City   New Delhi   Hong Kong   Buenos Aires

First published in Germany as *Gespensterjäger in großer Gefahr* by Loewe Verlag
Original text copyright © 2001 by Loewe Verlag
English translation by Helena Ragg-Kirkby copyright © 2007 by Cornelia Funke

Published in the United Kingdom in 2007 by The Chicken House,
2 Palmer Street, Frome, Somerset BA11 1DS.
www.doublecluck.com

Interior illustrations copyright © 2007 by Cornelia Funke

Library of Congress Cataloging-in-Publication Data Available

ISBN 13: 978-0-439-86269-1
ISBN 10: 0-439-86269-8

12 11 10 9 8 7 6 5 4 3 2 1   7 8 9 10 11 12/0

Printed in the U.S.A.   40
First Scholastic paperback printing, April 2007
The text type was set in Berthold Baskerville Book.
The display type was set in P22 Kane, Mister Frisky, and Zsazsa Galore.
Book design by Leyah Jensen

For
Elmar,
Andre,
and
Henri

CONTENTS

TOM | HUGO the ASG | HETTY

Let me introduce three of the most successful ghosthunters of our time.

The trio depicted above are three of the most famous ghosthunters of our time: Hetty Hyssop, Tom, and Hugo, a so-called **ASG** or **A**veragely **S**pooky **G**host. They call themselves *Hyssop & Co.* – and up until now they've successfully completed every one of their missions, though all of them were extremely challenging, even for such experienced ghosthunters as our three friends.

Their missions included fighting some of the most dangerous ghosts: an **IRG** (**I**ncredibly **R**evolting **G**host), who had already deep-frozen a client of theirs; a **GILIG** (**G**ruesome **I**nvincible **LI**ghtning **G**host), who had turned several of its victims into Fire Ghosts, before *Hyssop & Co.* took care of it; and – perhaps their most difficult job – the Totally Moldy Baroness, a particularly vicious **HIGA** (**HI**storical **G**hostly **A**pparition) whom Tom managed to defeat only by risking his own life.

After this adventure, the threesome had hoped it would be a while before things turned *that* bad again. But only a few months later they were to discover otherwise. It wasn't a mission that almost sealed their fate, though: It was Tom's **G**host**H**unting **D**iploma (**GHD**). And the field test didn't *sound* too difficult at all. . . .

One more thing: I would ask all readers who want to devour *Hyssop & Co.*'s fourth adventure to put it carefully aside when dusk falls. I would also recommend you not to read it in lonely, mist-shrouded places. But enough of this introduction.

It all began on a Friday in late March. It is well known that fateful events nearly always begin on a Friday. . . .

An Easy Task

L ater on, Tom would tell himself that his suspicions should have been aroused when he entered the huge, dimly lit office of Professor Slimeblott. Tom normally had a good nose for imminent danger. But on this occasion it failed him miserably.

"Sit down, Tom," said the professor, taking a swig from his coffee mug. Professor Slimeblott had only been on the **G**host**H**unting **AS**sociation's **E**xamining **B**oard for a month, and Tom had never met him before.

"You're the boy who works with Hetty Hyssop, aren't you?" he asked.

Tom nodded. The professor's eyes were strangely light, almost colorless, like everything else about him. Even his skin was as pale as faded paper, and his sparse hair, combed sideways across his bald head, was the same color as dried-out mud. *This guy reminds me of a* **PAWOG**, thought Tom. *Exactly the same cold and self-satisfied look.*

PAWOGs (**PA**le **WO**bbly **G**hosts) are best fought off with laughing gas, and Tom had to suppress a grin as he thought of it.

Slimeblott inspected him with his colorless eyes. "Does Hetty still work with that foolish ASG?" he asked.

"Of course," answered Tom, frowning. He didn't like people insulting his friends. Although it was true that Hugo could be very foolish.

"Well, I hope that the **CE**ntral **CO**mmission for **CO**mbating **G**hosts will put a stop to collaborating with ghosts this year," said the professor, drumming on the desk with a golden letter opener. "We're supposed to chase and destroy ghosts: That's our sole and honorable task. Ghosts are bent on harming humans: They envy us our bodies as well as our poor souls, which they destroy . . . mutilate . . . devour." As he said these last words, the professor's voice began to tremble, and he thrust the letter opener into his wooden desk with such force that it remained upright. When he noticed Tom's surprised expression, he quickly put the letter opener to one side, cleared his throat, and took another swig from his coffee mug.

"Well. Right, then. We'll leave it there, and move

on to your diploma, Tom," he said. "I must be honest and say that I think you are much too young to be taking final exams. The GhostHunting Diploma is normally earned by very experienced ghosthunters only. And you are, if my information is correct, a mere eleven years old."

Tom turned bright red with annoyance. "That's true," he said. "But when all's said and done, it only involves a Danger Category Three ghost."

"'Only.' Well, well," said the professor. "You certainly don't seem to lack self-confidence. You must be aware that this category also includes several extremely dangerous ghosts?"

"Yes, but they're not that difficult to fight," answered Tom. "And anyway, the only thing I haven't done yet is the field test: identifying and catching an unclassified ghost."

It's always the same! he thought. *People discover you're a bit younger than normal, and they all start acting as if you couldn't tell the difference between an ASG and an IRG.*

(Gentle reader: ASG = Averagely Spooky Ghost; IRG = Incredibly Revolting Ghost, in case you imprudently skipped the introduction to delve straight into the story.)

The professor sighed, leaned back in his chair, and allowed his pale gaze to wander along the walls of his office. Much to Tom's surprise, they weren't red. Most ghosthunters choose this color because it scares off ghosts. But Slimeblott's office had dark blue walls. Dozens of framed newspaper clippings hung on them, trumpeting his triumphs in the ghosthunting field.

"Well, I can see that you are quite determined," said the professor, letting his gaze wander back to Tom. "Have it your way. Presumably you know the basic rules?"

For a moment, Tom thought he could see something close to malice in the colorless eyes.

"Of course," he answered. "I have to catch the ghost single-handed, but I can choose two, maximum three, helpers to observe it and to lure it in. . . ."

"One," the professor corrected him.

"One?" Tom looked at him, surprised. "I thought —"

"Well, the examinations board has tightened up the regulations somewhat," the professor interrupted him. "At my suggestion."

Tom just managed to swallow a quiet curse. How was he supposed to explain this to Hugo?

"And what's more," the professor continued with a nasty chuckle, "to fulfill your task, you may only use equipment that is listed in the **GhostHUnting GuideLines**. Special pastes and invented tools of the kind that our colleague Hyssop likes to use are not allowed. If you rely on those, you will be deemed to have failed."

Tom just nodded. He had been expecting this.

"Good. Now to the task itself." Professor Slimeblott cleared his throat and opened a slim file. "The ghostly apparition you will be dealing with was reported three days ago in a village named Bogpool, about a hundred miles northeast of here. The owner of the village's only inn has already been informed that you will be staying there and will need a double room. Here is the full address along with travel directions and a brief summary of your mission."

The professor handed Tom a sealed envelope bearing the **GhostHunting Association's** stamp. Tom scanned the summary:

YOU MUST SUBMIT THE FOLLOWING TO THE GHOSTHUNTING ASSOCIATION'S EXAMINATIONS BOARD:

Firstly: *a precise report on all the ghostly activity you have observed (two copies, typed).*

Secondly: *sound recordings, photos, and/or filmed material of the ghostly apparition (thermospiritist recordings are, of course, permitted).*

Thirdly: *the ghostly specimen, captured and unharmed. We recommend that you use a COCOT (COntact-COmpression Trap); using these on Danger Category Three ghosts involves the least risk.*

Tom nodded. As if he needed to have that explained to him. Didn't this pesky committee realize that, as a member of Hyssop & Co., he'd already caught Category Six ghosts?

"Anything else?" asked Tom, stuffing the envelope containing his exam task into his backpack.

"Well, I hope you have a successful hunt," answered the professor. "Or how do ghosthunters put it? 'Keep your head, even after midnight.'"

There was something about Professor Slimeblott's voice that Tom didn't like at all, but before he could give it any further thought, Slimeblott held out his hand to him with a thin laugh.

The professor's fingers were almost as cold as Hugo's.

"Good luck, Tom!" he said. "And send Hetty Hyssop my regards."

"Will do," replied Tom, and shook the chalk-white hand as firmly as possible. "I'd estimate I'll have it all wrapped up by the end of next week."

"Oh yes?" said Slimeblott. "You really are a quick worker, aren't you, Tom?" Then he smiled again. And Tom noticed that even the professor's lips were completely colorless.

The Village in the Fog

Hugo turned as green as moldy bread when Tom told him that he and Hetty Hyssop would be going to Bogpool alone.

"So, soooooooo. They only alloooow one helper!" he breathed, folding his arms across his pale chest. "Well, then, leave Hetty here."

"Oh, right, so *you're* going to drive me to this village, are you?" Tom retorted crossly.

Hugo wrinkled up his big white nose. "Car? Pah! Whooooo needs a car? Weeeee'll fly!"

"No!" Tom said firmly. "No, not again. Out of the question."

Hugo had already carried him over roofs and the tops of trees, and the speed at which the ASG traveled always took Tom's breath away.

"And anyway," Tom added, "Hetty can help me with my report. The best you'd manage would be to make my computer keyboard all slimy."

He shouldn't have said that. Hugo angrily blew his moldy breath into Tom's face — and vanished through the wall. Later that evening, when Tom went to pack his backpack for the journey, he plunged his hand into greeny-yellow, disgustingly sticky ASG slime.

Having a ghost for a friend really could be exhausting at times.

The next day, Hetty Hyssop picked up Tom bang on time at five-thirty in the afternoon. They wanted to arrive at Bogpool at night, so that Tom wouldn't have to wait too long to see a ghost. When all's said and done, ninety-six percent of ghostly apparitions appear only when it's dark.

"I think you've got your diploma pretty much in the bag already," said Hetty Hyssop as they drove down an infinitely long, infinitely straight country road. "Danger Category Three ghosts are sometimes inclined to play hideous tricks, but they shouldn't be a problem for a ghosthunter with your experience."

"That's what I figure, too," muttered Tom, fishing a dinner roll out of his backpack. He wasn't hungry, but every experienced ghosthunter has something to eat before getting down to work. There are some things you can withstand better if you have a full stomach — that dreadful prickling, for example, that you feel when ghosts float through you. (The smaller **SW**ig **G**hosts particularly like doing this.)

"What bothers me the most is having to type up the report," said Tom, biting into his roll with no enthusiasm. "And Hugo . . . he really was pretty offended about not being allowed to come with us."

"Oh well. ASGs are permanently offended," Hetty Hyssop replied. "You should know that by now."

"True," said Tom, brushing a couple of crumbs off his pants. The last time he'd quarreled with the ASG, Hugo had been offended for thirteen days and had howled outside Tom's window every night.

"Maybe I could bring something back for him," murmured Tom. "But what do you give a ghost?"

Thoughtfully, he looked out the car window. The landscape was gray and monotonous. The sky above the bare fields was full of heavy clouds, and there wasn't a house to be seen for miles. The pallid gray ponds reflected the bare trees, and there was no hint of spring in the air even though it was already the end of March.

"When I look at this area, it seems to me that you're likely to be dealing with a **BOSG** or a **FOFIFO**," said Hetty Hyssop.

"Very likely," said Tom. "They often do their haunting in dismal, damp places like this."

(Gentle reader: BOSG = **BO**g and **S**wamp **G**host. FOFIFO = **FO**ggy **FI**gure **FO**rmer.)

Hetty Hyssop steered around a huge puddle in the road. "Who assigned you this mission?" she asked. "Professor Eatitall?"

A solitary church steeple appeared on the horizon.

Tom shook his head. "No. This guy's new to the examinations board. He's a nasty piece of work: Professor Slimeblott."

Hetty Hyssop swung around to Tom so abruptly that she almost ran into a road sign. Just in time, she stepped on the brake. "Slimeblott?" she asked, steering her old sedan to the curb. "Lotan Slimeblott?"

"No idea what his first name is," answered Tom, looking at her in surprise. "What's wrong with him?"

Hetty Hyssop kneaded the tip of her nose. Then she shook her head and restarted the engine. "Oh well!" she said. "I'm sure it doesn't mean anything. All that business was many years ago, after all."

"What business?" asked Tom.

"Oh, Slimeblott and I once had a terrible row about fighting **SLU**rp **G**hosts. He was absolutely desperate to prove to me how effective his method was. But the ghost he picked a quarrel with would have slurped him up like a cup of cold coffee if I hadn't intervened. Slimeblott took it pretty badly."

"Well, that's pretty ungrateful," said Tom – and had to grin. "The professor doesn't *look* much like coffee," he remarked. "More like a glass of skim milk."

Hetty Hyssop laughed pointedly. "Well, you know what encountering a Slurper can do to you. Some victims are as white as paper tissues for the rest of their lives. Gracious! Seeing your dinner roll really makes me feel hungry. With a bit of luck, Slimeblott will have booked us into an inn where we can get something decent to eat."

Dusk was already falling when they reached Bogpool. The streets were shrouded in fog and the first houses in the village emerged like shadows from the mist. Bogpool was an old village, so old that it felt to Tom as if the fog had once swallowed it up and then spat it out again from some bygone era.

A narrow cobbled street led directly to the big church. It stood in the middle of the village, surrounded by an empty square with houses crowding around it as if they were seeking protection in the shadow of the huge steeple. Only very few lights were on.

"Not very inviting, is it?" Tom remarked as Hetty Hyssop parked her car opposite the church.

Shivering, they got out of the car and looked around them. The place was completely silent, as if it were deserted. Not even a stray cat moved amongst the houses.

"I can just imagine what Hugo would say now," said Tom. "Ooooooh, what a wonderfuuuul place to go spooooooking!"

Hetty Hyssop smiled. "Very likely. What was the address of that inn again?"

Tom strolled to the trunk of the car. "I'll have a look," he said.

The sky was becoming darker and darker, and above the houses the fog merged with the smoke that rose from the chimneys. *Well, this is ghostly weather and a half!* thought Tom, reaching for the handle of the car trunk. His fingers got stuck on it — and he immediately knew what *that* meant.

Angrily he wrenched the trunk open. "Come out!" he cried. "Come on out, you devious slimy creep of an ASG!"

A pale hand cautiously slid its way up between the suitcases. "OK, OK!" breathed Hugo. "Iiiiiii'm coooooooming."

"Thank your lucky stars I've not got any eggs on me!" shouted Tom. "But I'm sure I'll find a bit of salt, you —"

Hugo's hand vanished back between the suitcases with a jerk. "Eggs! Salt!" he grouched in a muffled voice. "Is that any way to greeeeeet yoooour friends?"

(For the information of readers with no experience of ghosts: Salt is almost as painful to ASGs as hydrochloric acid is to human skin.)

"Come on out, you silly old ASG," said Hetty Hyssop, coming to stand next to Tom. "Tom doesn't mean it."

"Oh no?" cried Tom angrily. "If that Slimeblott finds out I've had two helpers with me, I can forget all about my diploma!"

"OK, OK! Iiiii won't lift an icy finger tooooo help yoooooou!" moaned Hugo, floating out of his hiding place. "Ghost's unholy honor!"

Tom turned his back on him contemptuously. Cursing, he opened his sticky suitcase and fished out the envelope Professor Slimeblott had given him.

"Three Old Village Street," read Hetty Hyssop, looking around. "That's presumably just behind there." She turned to go, pulling Hugo along with her, but Tom didn't follow.

"Wait a sec," he answered. "I'll just have a quick look at the church. Looks like a place that might appeal to ghosts."

"Yes, I thought so, too," said Hetty Hyssop, staring up at the heavy steeple. The big hand on the clock was just coming up to the twelve. They could hear it clicking from down on the ground.

"It doesn't smell goooooood!" breathed Hugo, floating to Tom's side. "Oh no. Not gooooood at all!"

"Just get lost in the backpack, for goodness' sake!" Tom snapped at him. "I don't want anyone to see you. Can't you get it into your pale skull? If Slimeblott finds out about you, I've had it!"

"Yeah, yeah!" breathed Hugo, offended, and squeezed himself into the backpack, which was already stuffed full. "I ooooonly wanted tooooo help."

"But you *shouldn't* help me!" hissed Tom over his

shoulder. "Have you already taken your **G**hostly **E**nergy **A**nti-**S**ensor?"

"Of coourse!" breathed Hugo. "Though it gives yooooou a terribly tickly throoooat." (Hetty Hyssop had invented the GEAS especially for Hugo. It was hardly any bigger than a sucking candy, but it made sure that the ghosthunters' devices didn't go off when Hugo went near them.)

"Oh good. Well, *that's* something, at least," growled Tom. "And woe betide you if you slime everything up in there again." Then he took his **G**hostly **E**nergy **S**ensor out of his jacket pocket and walked side by side with Hetty Hyssop to the church. "Bingo!" he said as the needle started to quiver.

(Gentle reader: People who don't know anything about ghosthunting mostly mistake the GES for an alarm clock with four fingers.)

"Clear traces of ghostly energy," Tom announced. "I'd say the ghost was at work here the whole of last night. With a bit of luck, we'll get another look at him tonight!"

"Entirely possible," said Hetty Hyssop. "Category Three ghosts are often out haunting every night. And it's absolutely fantastic for you, Tom, that he's chosen a church. You can make great sound recordings in churches. They give all the howling and moaning a nice little echo."

Hugo's head poked slightly out of Tom's backpack. "If Iiiiii coould just say soooomething," he breathed. "Iiiiii . . . "

"One more word," growled Tom, "and I'll get my saltshaker. Do you know what the punishment is for breaking a ghost's unholy honor?"

But Hugo had already disappeared.

Hetty Hyssop suppressed a smile. "Good!" she said, turning away from the church. "Let's get to that inn. We need to get our strength up; it might be a turbulent night."

"Let's hope so," said Tom, putting away his GES. As he took a last look around, a strange feeling of discomfort crept across his limbs — as if he were a mouse who had run into a trap without realizing it and suddenly heard it snapping shut on him.

"Snap!" muttered Tom, looking again at the church steeple looming high above them.

"What did you say?" asked Hetty Hyssop.

"Oh, nothing," murmured Tom — and raised his head, listening carefully. A peculiar hissing sound was coming from somewhere and penetrating his ear. It sounded sharp and threatening.

"Careful, Tom!" cried Hetty Hyssop, and made a lunge for him.

But Hugo was quicker. He shot out of the backpack, grabbed Tom with his icy arms, and whisked him up into the air. As he did so, the hour hand of the clock plunged down and bored its way into the ground in front of the church. Quivering, it lodged itself between the stones in exactly the place where Tom had just been standing.

"Someone's ooorganiiiiized a welcome committeeeee!" breathed Hugo, putting Tom back on his own two feet.

"That's a pretty violent way for a Category Three ghost to say hello," said Hetty Hyssop with a frown. "Oh well, I *thought* it was odd that there seem to be so few people in this village. But who knows what else this ghost has been dropping on people since it started getting up to mischief here."

Tom pushed his glasses straight. They had almost slipped off his ears, and his fingers were still trembling from the shock. "Thanks, Hugo!" he stammered. "That thing nearly speared me like a marshmallow!"

"Noooo worrieees!" breathed Hugo. "Although, of course, Iiiiii wasn't, in fact, supposed toooooo lift a fiiiinger."

"Oh, I see no reason to tell Professor Slimeblott about what happened," said Hetty Hyssop. "After all, Tom's not properly got down to work yet."

"Exactly," murmured Tom, staggering to the clock hand, his legs still wobbling. When he ran the GES across the rusty metal, it began to glow silver. Sparks shot out onto Tom's hand, as cold as snowflakes. "Well, there we have it," he said. "That thing definitely did not fall down by accident."

He looked up at the huge church windows. Behind them, he thought he could see something flickering. "You wait," he growled through clenched teeth. "I'll put a stop to your nasty jokes, you miserable whatever-you-are." He straightened his back and resolutely strode toward the church door, but Hetty Hyssop stood in his way.

"Leave it, Tom," she said, putting her arm around

his shoulders. "Anger isn't a good guide, and you've got no idea what's lurking in there."

Reluctantly, Tom let her pull him back toward the car. As he got in, he again thought he could see something flickering behind the dark church windows, something as pale as the fog that still hung over the houses.

Then it disappeared.

Hornheaver

The inn, the Final Round, was only a few yards from the church. Its walls were clad in a leafy cloak of ivy; even the windows were half covered. Only on the ground floor did light fall through the windowpane and out onto the fog-shrouded road.

"The Final Round?" grumbled Tom to Hetty before they opened the front door. "What kind of name is that supposed to be?"

Hugo was tucked in the backpack, in spite of his usual protests. After all, if people don't have much experience with ghosts, the sight of even a (relatively harmless) ASG is enough to make them pass out and stutter for days.

However, the innkeeper of the Final Round didn't look particularly easily scared. He was built like a brick outhouse.

"Hetty Hyssop and Tom?" he growled, as Hetty signed herself and Tom into the guest book (not mentioning Hugo). "Aha, so you're the ghosthunters. Well, we'll see whether you have better luck than your colleagues."

"Colleagues?" asked Hetty Hyssop, casting a surprised look at Tom.

"Oh yes, we've already had several ghosthunters stay here," said the innkeeper, banging the book shut. "This is the twelfth ghost we've reported to those ghost authorities. Curses, I can never remember their proper name."

"**ROGA**," said Tom. "**R**egister **O**ffice for **G**hostly Apparitions."

"Precisely!" growled the huge innkeeper.

"The twelfth one you've reported?" said Hetty Hyssop. "That really is something."

The innkeeper shrugged his shoulders. "Oh well, this village attracts ghosts the way that cow pies attract flies. Nobody knows why. Quite a lot of the houses here are already standing empty because of it."

"Really? Very interesting," said Hetty Hyssop. "Well, the ghost that we're here for is supposed to have appeared for the first time just a couple of days ago."

The innkeeper nodded and noisily blew his nose. (He had a nose that looked as if someone had squashed

it flat.) "Yes, one comes and another one goes. This new one gets up to its tricks mostly in the church and the vicarage. Although I've not had the pleasure myself, apparently it's as gray as roofing felt, this one."

"Gray?" Tom and Hetty quickly exchanged glances.

"Can you tell us anything about its haunting activities?" asked Tom, pushing up his glasses.

"'Haunting activities'? Well, you put it very nicely, don't you, laddie?" said the innkeeper, stuffing his handkerchief back in his pocket. "Hmm, well, it's supposed to throw stuff around. Does a lot of howling, too, it seems. And they say its screeching is truly ear-splitting. The vicar's sister looks pretty done in already."

"Really . . ." murmured Tom. He couldn't help but remember the hour hand. He suddenly felt sick. "Does it do anything else?" he asked.

"Well, you'd be better off asking the vicar and his sister. The vicarage is right behind the church." The innkeeper ran his fingers across his stubbly chin and pushed the room key across the counter to Hetty Hyssop. "Up the stairs. Second door on the left. Would you like me to bring you something to eat?"

"That would be very kind." Hetty Hyssop picked up her suitcase — and spotted Hugo's icy fingers, which were just about to write something in the guest book.

"Hugo!" she hissed, and the fingers disappeared back into Tom's backpack.

"Hugo? No, my name is Erwin. Erwin Hornheaver," growled the innkeeper. "How about poached egg and chips?"

"Without the egg, thanks," said Tom, dragging his luggage to the staircase that led up to the first floor. "Ghosts can smell you a mile off if you've been eating eggs."

"Well, I never!" growled Erwin, looking at him in astonishment. "Pretty young to be a ghosthunter, the little lad, isn't he?" he whispered to Hetty Hyssop.

"That's Tom − a first-class ghosthunter, my dear man," replied Hetty Hyssop. "He has already taken on ghosts the mere sight of which would turn you to dust before you could say 'egg and chips.'"

Then she followed Tom up the steep, creaky staircase. When she turned around once more, she saw Erwin Hornheaver watching them, surprise written all over his face.

The chips were delicious. Tom tipped a great load of chili and garlic powder over them so that he and Hetty would smell unappetizing to ghosts that night − which meant that Hugo had to stick a clothespin on his pale nose.

"Gray!" mused Tom as he speared his last chip. "That covers loads of different types of ghost. D'you think it might be a negative projection?"

Hetty Hyssop shrugged her shoulders. "It's not likely, but you ought to be prepared for it," she said.

Tom pushed his plate aside and spread out his equipment on the bed. "Hugo, we don't know when we'll get back from the vicarage. The ghost might appear when we're talking to the vicar and his sister. Nobody knows better than you how much ghosts like to appear when people are discussing them. But however long we're gone, you're to stay in this room — got it?"

"Why? I'll be booooored to death!" groaned Hugo, slumping down on the windowsill.

"Don't talk nonsense — you're already dead," said Hetty Hyssop. "And get away from the window."

With a defiant expression, Hugo leaned his pale back against the cool glass. "But there's such a looooovely draft here," he groused.

Irritated, Hetty Hyssop pushed him aside and closed the curtains. Tom stood in front of the bed, frowning as he sorted out the equipment he wanted to take with him.

"You really should use the **HY**per-**SO**und **F**ilters," said Hetty Hyssop. "To judge by what Hornheaver said, we might be dealing with a screecher."

"I've already put them behind my ears," said Tom.

(Gentle reader: Screechers are ghosts who make straight for their victims, screeching so penetratingly that they even bend metal objects. It had happened to Tom once, and he'd been stone-deaf for thirteen days afterward. Since then, he always wore **HYOSF**s behind his ears when he went on missions.)

"And have you got your **NE**gative-**NE**utralizer **B**elt on?" asked Hetty Hyssop, tossing Tom his protective helmet.

"Yep, check, the **NENEB** is on," he answered, donning the helmet and lifting up his sweater. A broad black belt was slung around his hips. A net of silver thread reached up from it to his chest.

"Excellent," said Hetty Hyssop. "What about your camera?"

"Ready to shoot," said Tom. "I've got my dictaphone as well. Recording what the vicar tells us is bound to be useful for my report."

"Can't I at least scaaaaare our fat landlooooord?" Hugo called after them as they were already standing in the door.

"Don't you dare!" said Tom, and closed the bedroom door behind him.

Ghostly Visit

It was dark outside now, but the fog still hung in white streamers between the houses. There was nobody around as Tom and Hetty Hyssop crossed the church square. Their steps echoed on the damp paving stones, and a dog barked somewhere. The air smelled strangely musty, as if someone had stuffed it into a preserving jar and let it out again a thousand years later. As they passed the church, Tom's head turned automatically to look at it. The windows were dark, and up on the church steeple clock, the minute hand was doing its lonely round.

They found the vicarage right behind the church, just where Erwin Hornheaver had said it would be. It was hidden behind a high wall covered in dense foliage. The wrought-iron gate was open a crack, and the path that led to the house was so muddy that the ground squelched beneath Tom's boots. The house itself looked strangely crooked, as if it were bending down toward the dirt. A light was on in one of the windows on the ground floor. It glowed brightly in the gathering gloom.

"Oh, fantastic, someone's at home!" whispered Tom, pressing the bell. "But who on Earth built this house? Looks as if it's about to fall down any minute."

Hetty Hyssop didn't answer. She poked her umbrella into the flower bed next to the front door, held the tip up to her nose, and sniffed it. "The same musty smell that's in the air," she mused. "Strange. Does it say anything to you?"

"Well, it doesn't seem as if we're dealing with a Bog and Swamp Ghost," replied Tom. "As far as I remember, *they* make everything smell of lilies. But here it stinks like someone's airing out an old crypt."

At that moment, the vicarage door opened. A little old lady as thin as a stick of asparagus brandished a poker at them threateningly. "What do you want?" she asked brusquely.

Her face wasn't particularly pale, but her earlobes trembled and her eyebrows kept twitching nervously upward as if they wanted to run away. Clearly the result of ghostly encounters, as Tom recognized only too well.

"Good evening," said Hetty Hyssop, pushing the poker aside with a friendly smile. "My name is Hetty Hyssop, and this is my colleague, Tom. We're ghost-hunters, and we'd very much like to have a chat with you about the ghostly apparition that's been visiting you for the last few days."

The skinny little woman jumped so violently that three bobby pins slipped out of her icy gray bun. She screwed up her eyes and looked around; then she listened into the brightly lit house behind her — and bent down to the pair of ghosthunters. "This village is cursed!" she whispered, thrusting the poker at Tom's chest. "Go home, quickly! We should all leave, but nobody listens to me, not even my own brother!"

At that very moment the light went off behind her. With one fell swoop all the windows of the house went dark, and a deep sigh came from the open front door. It stroked Tom's face like the damp breath of an invisible animal.

"May I?" Tom said, and moved the little woman and her poker to one side. Then he quickly entered the pitch-dark house with Hetty Hyssop close behind. A couple of steps across a narrow hallway, and the two were standing in, as far as Tom could make out in the darkness, the living room. "I think we'll need the magnetizer!" he whispered to Hetty Hyssop.

"Good idea!" she whispered back.

Tom clasped his backpack between his legs and pulled a horseshoe-shaped object out of it. Hetty Hyssop was already holding her magnetizer.

"Go outside!" Tom told the little old lady when she appeared in the doorway. "Things will get pretty unpleasant in here in a minute!"

Something was bumping and banging above his head, and he could hear steps, heavy and irregular.

"Into position, Tom!" cried Hetty Hyssop, standing exactly four paces away from him and aiming her **GHO**st **M**agnetizer at the ceiling.

"It's resisting!" cried Tom as his magnetizer began to hum like an angry wasp. "I'm switching mine to full force!"

"Agreed!" cried Hetty Hyssop.

A fierce screech resounded above their heads, and suddenly something fell through the ceiling. With a dull thud, it landed on the carpet in front of them.

"A **NEPGA**!" cried Tom. He hastily threw his magnetizer onto the ground and pressed the buckle of his NENEB. The ghost stood up, panting, and remained

35

cowering in the middle of the room. It shimmered gray in the darkness; its shape was outlined by a blaze of light; and it radiated icy coldness.

Tom had read several things about **NE**gative **P**rojections of a **G**hostly **A**pparition, but he'd never come face-to-face with one in person. The NEPGA took a human form, but it didn't glow pale white like most ghosts do, being instead the color of dirty smoke. Its blazing outline pulsated as if blood were still flowing through its ghostly veins. But the spookiest thing about it was its face. It looked like the negative of a black-and-white photo.

The pale eyes made Tom shudder. Their pupils were an icy white color and they bored into Tom's face like pins.

"Come on, concentrate, Tom!" he muttered to himself, not letting the NEPGA out of his sight for a second. "Think of your diploma. Take a picture of this monster!"

It took his fingers a moment, though, to obey his thoughts and pull the tiny special camera out of his pocket. Tom managed to press the button only once before the NEPGA whizzed into the air and floated toward him, its arms outstretched. As an experienced

ghosthunter, Tom knew only too well that any
unprotected contact with a NEPGA had extremely
painful consequences for living beings, but he didn't
move a muscle.

"Yooou've had it!" breathed the ghost in a voice
that came from the very depths of its body. Then

it poked a smoky gray finger at Tom's chest — and froze.

"Ha, that surprised you, didn't it?" Tom grabbed the NEPGA's arm before it could get over its shock that its victim had not doubled over with pain.

"That business with the clock hand," Tom continued. "I really took that personally. What a mean-*spirited* joke. You can be sure I will get a lot of pleasure out of putting you in a nice cozy — "

Sadly he didn't get any further. Someone shoved him aside so violently that he let go of the ghost's arm. With a cry, the vicar's sister pushed past Tom. "You miserable, revolting, glass-shattering *thing*!" she yelled. And before Tom or Hetty Hyssop could stop her, she walloped the NEPGA on the head with her poker. The poker immediately turned as floppy as a stick of licorice. The ghost, however, floated past Tom with an evil laugh and disappeared out the door and into the foggy night.

"Curses!" shouted Tom. "Curses — I had it!"

"No time for self-pity. I bet it's fled to the church!" said Hetty Hyssop, thrusting Tom's backpack into his hand.

"Don't get involved any more if you value your life!" she shouted to the little old lady before following Tom outside.

"But my brother!" the lady cried shrilly after them. "My brother's in the church!"

"Oh, great, we really needed that on top of everything else!" groaned Tom. "Isn't there anyplace around here where you can catch a ghost in peace and quiet?"

The Twelfth Messenger

There was no sign of the NEPGA when Tom and Hetty Hyssop arrived at the church door. However, Tom's GES was quivering unmistakably, so there was no doubting where the ghost had fled to.

"I must admit, I got a real shock when that monster touched you," whispered Hetty Hyssop as Tom pressed an ear to the church door to hear what was going on inside. "But we certainly can rely on you to keep your head, Tom."

"Oh well, all I had to do was press the buckle of my neutralizer belt," murmured Tom, embarrassed. "But it does feel unpleasantly prickly when the protective shield goes up. As if about five thousand ants were scrabbling all over you!"

"Well, it's probably even more unpleasant spending fourteen days racked by muscle cramps," Hetty Hyssop whispered back. "And that's the least of the side effects caused by being in contact with one of those hideous things. Do you hear anything?"

"No. Not a single sigh." Tom removed his ear from the door and reached for the door handle, but Hetty Hyssop stopped him.

"Just wait another minute," she whispered. "I've had lots of dealings with NEPGAs, and there doesn't seem to be anything unusual about this one at first sight, but . . ."

Tom completed her sentence. ". . . Negative Projections of ghosts only appear in places with an unusually strong magico-spiritual energy field. And" – he looked thoughtfully up at the dark church walls – "this church somehow doesn't look like that sort of place."

"No, it certainly doesn't!" whispered Hetty, running the handle of her umbrella across the stone wall. Tom had often seen the handle start to glow like a lightbulb, but this time nothing happened at all. "No sign!" said Hetty quietly. "This building is as harmless as a bus stop. A home best suited to a gentle local ghost. So where's the NEPGA getting its energy from?"

Tom shrugged his shoulders, at a loss. "Let's think about it later," he said. "It's not something I need to know for my diploma. But I've got to catch this sneaky clock-hand hurler if I want to get my certificate."

Hetty Hyssop sighed. "Yes, you're right, let's concentrate on your assigned task. Maybe the ghost will provide a couple of the answers itself. Have you got the trap handy?"

Tom carefully pulled a sphere out of his jacket pocket. It was as clear as glass and slightly bigger than a tennis ball. "Yep, got it," he said, and let it slip back into his pocket. Then he took a deep breath once again – and pushed open the heavy door.

The air that met them was cold and damp, and Tom inhaled the same musty smell that they had already noticed outside. The large door slammed shut behind them with a muffled bang, and darkness enveloped them. The only light came from a couple of candles that flickered at the feet of a marble saint. Carefully the two ghosthunters stepped between the empty rows of benches.

"No sign of any vicar!" whispered Tom, straining to see in the dim space. "And no sign of the NEPGA, either. Blasted nuisance that it's such a dark color."

But at that very moment, he saw the ghost.

Flickering, it floated up between two pillars directly under the soot-blackened vault of the church. The only thing that gave it away was its glowing silhouette. As soon as Tom looked up, it sank down again with a sigh — as if it had *felt* Tom's gaze (not unusual for ghosts). It hung in the air barely ten feet above Tom's head, staring down at the ghosthunters with its white eyes and moaning so deeply that several of the candles flickered and went out.

"Here we go!" whispered Hetty Hyssop, pointing her magnetizer at the NEPGA. Immediately it began to tremble like a piece of paper being sucked up by a vacuum cleaner, and sank even lower.

Tom thrust his hand into his jacket pocket.

"Ready," he said. Hetty switched off the magnetizer and took a couple of paces backward. According to the rules of the field test, Tom had to do the rest on his own. No further help was permitted. He had to capture the ghost single-handedly. And Tom knew exactly how to lure a NEPGA into a trap. It was just a question of finding the right words. You caught these kinds of ghosts by insulting them.

"Now listen to me, you white-eyed, gray, papery thing!" Tom cried up to the floating ghost. "I've never

seen anything like you before. Are you a scrap of ancient carbon paper or a badly lit photograph?"

The NEPGA emitted an angry growl and sank down even farther. The cold that radiated from it made Tom shiver, and the "ants" prickled his skin again.

"No, hang on a sec!" he cried. "I've got it. Some **Fire Ghost** played a trick on you and turned you into a little piece of sooty paper! A pretty bad joke, if you ask me."

The ghost gave a shriek that made the candlesticks on the altar melt like hot wax.

Now! thought Tom, rubbing his aching ears. *I've nearly done it! Any minute now, he'll come after me.* The Contact-Compression Trap felt pleasantly warm when Tom pulled it out of his pocket. He'd passed his COCOT-throwing exam with a B-plus, just two misthrows out of fifteen. But now just *one* misthrow could have extremely painful consequences.

The NEPGA floated above him, as gray as a thundercloud, and stared at him with its spooky eyes.

"Oh, what am I talking about!" cried Tom. "*Now* I've got it. You're just a piece of completely crazy roofing felt!"

The ghost snarled so angrily that Tom's hair stood

on end like the quills on a porcupine. But it still didn't come down. Curses. What was going on?

"I'm the Tweeelfth Messsengeeeeer!" came from its white mouth.

Flummoxed, Tom looked over at Hetty Hyssop. But she looked back, equally puzzled.

"The Twelfth Messenger?" cried Tom. "Who from?"

"Heee'll destrooooooooooy you!" cried the ghost.

"Who, for goodness' sake?" Tom cried back.

But the NEPGA didn't reply. It opened its mouth wide, so wide that Tom could see all its teeth, and let out such a hideous screech that Tom's eardrums almost burst despite the Hyper-Sound Filter. Then the ghost stretched its dark fingers out to Tom — and plunged down upon him like a shadow.

At the same moment, Tom threw the trap. And he didn't miss.

With a sharp hissing sound, the ball disappeared into the dark shape of the NEPGA — and the ghost vanished. The COCOT trap, however, reappeared, dropped onto the church floor, and rolled down the aisle between the benches until it stopped by the steps leading to the altar.

Breathing a sigh of relief, Hetty Hyssop came to stand by Tom's side and put her arm around his shoulders. "Fantastic throw, my dear boy," she said. "I've never seen a better one."

"Oh, um, well," murmured Tom, bending his head to hide his proud smile. Then he ran over to the ghost trap and picked it up. The NEPGA was stuck inside like a fly in amber. And it was looking pretty dazed, as far as anyone could tell with a Negative Projection!

"Do you have to find out what century it's from for your report?" asked Hetty Hyssop.

"No, thank goodness," said Tom, and yawned. All of a sudden he was terribly tired.

"It obviously hasn't done much damage," said Hetty Hyssop, looking around. "That statue over there has lost its head, and it seems to have thrown the pulpit around a bit, but everything else looks in reasonable shape. I just wonder where the vicar's got to."

"Maybe he made the great mistake of shaking his spooky visitor's hand," mused Tom, yawning again. "If the NEPGA really got ahold of him, the vicar will be lying around as stiff as a board somewhere, and he won't stir again for a month, at the earliest."

"Entirely possible," said Hetty Hyssop. "But

sometimes the victims can at least tell us something. Hello?" she cried into the dark church. "Is anyone there?" Her voice echoed around the vault as if it were wandering from pillar to pillar.

There was no reply, and Tom and Hetty Hyssop were just about to have a rather more thorough look for the missing vicar when they suddenly heard a faint voice coming from behind the altar.

"Hello?" A small, white-haired man peeped cautiously over the altar.

"You can come out!" cried Tom, holding up the trap. "We've caught the ghost. Your church is spook-free again!"

"Oh, really?" cried the vicar, standing up hesitantly. He was barely visible in his black garb. Only his white hair and chalky face showed up in the darkness. "It threw candlesticks around!" he cried, his legs wobbling as he came hurrying down the altar steps. "It pulled off Saint Anthony's head. And all it left of Saint Brigitta was a load of wood shavings."

"Well, consider yourself lucky that it didn't amuse itself with you," Tom remarked, putting the trap with his ghostly catch into his jacket pocket.

"Wh–wh–why, young man? What would have happened?" stammered the vicar.

"Well, first of all, it's incredibly painful if a ghost of that species touches you," Tom explained. "And then you go as stiff as a board – or as stiff as one of your marble saints – for at least a month."

The vicar looked at him, horrified. "Really?" he breathed.

"One hundred percent true," said Tom, yawning

once again as he turned away. He really just wanted to go to bed.

"Have a nice evening," Hetty Hyssop called back to the vicar, who looked completely shattered. "Say hello to your sister from us, and do tell her that the ghost won't be bothering her anymore."

"Um, yes, er, of course!" the vicar called after them. "But how do you know my sister?"

"Oh, she'll tell you all about that," replied Tom, and shut the heavy church door behind them.

Suspicious Holes

"The Twelfth Messenger," mused Tom as he and Hetty were making their way back to the inn. "What on Earth did the NEPGA mean by that?"

"That's what I'd like to know, too," replied Hetty Hyssop. "I think we should ask your computer a few questions tomorrow morning. My goodness, this fog's getting thicker and thicker!"

Tom had noticed that, too. The musty smell had also become stronger. It was almost enough to make you sick. And the really strange thing was, the houses in the village seemed to moan quietly to themselves, as if the old walls had come to life and were groaning under the weight of a too heavy burden.

"Now what does *that* mean?" said Tom, stopping. "Have you ever heard anything like it?"

Hetty raised her head and listened closely. "Yes, that does sound very strange," she said. "But whatever else is going on in this village, you've done the job we came here for. Gracious, are you as tired as I am?"

Tom yawned. "Too right I am," he said, strolling along. "I once read it's a side effect of coming into contact with Negative Projections."

"Yes, that's what they say," said Hetty Hyssop, also yawning. "But I've never experienced it to this extent before. If it were only me, I'd think it was because I'm getting old, but since it's just the same for you . . ."

She turned onto the narrow street that housed Erwin Hornheaver's inn — and stopped as if rooted to the spot. "By the moldy breath of an ASG, what's happened here?" she burst out.

"Good grief!" muttered Tom, staring at the street in bewilderment. The cobbles had developed peculiar lumps and bumps, and there were stones missing everywhere, as if the ground had swallowed them up.

Hetty Hyssop stuck her umbrella into one of the holes and poked around in it. "Mud," she said. "Nothing but mud. Like outside the vicarage. We need to ask Hornheaver if it's rained more than usual recently. If not . . ." She didn't finish her sentence.

"If not, then what?" asked Tom, disconcerted.

But Hetty Hyssop just shook her head. "If only I knew . . ."

Once they were inside the inn, they couldn't find their host anywhere. Erwin Hornheaver evidently went to bed early. But a note was stuck to their door.

"Hugo!" Tom sighed.

Hetty Hyssop unlocked the door and flicked on the light. There was no sign of the ASG. "Of course. First he made a commotion here, and then he slipped off," she said, irritated. "He's probably up to all kinds of stupid tricks again. But we really have got better things to worry about than looking after a silly ASG."

Strange noises in your room. Door wouldn't open. Are you keeping an elephant in there?!
—Erwin Hornheaver

"I'd feel happier if we knew more precisely what it is that we're worrying about," said Tom, putting the COCOT with its ghastly prisoner into an empty ashtray. Then, yawning, he crouched in front of the glassy ball and watched the ghost carefully. "So, we've identified, photographed, and caught it," he said. "And the report shouldn't be a problem if we get a bit more information out of the vicar and his sister tomorrow

about the haunting in the vicarage. After that, we can, theoretically, go home."

Hetty Hyssop just nodded. She was looking out the window, kneading the tip of her pointy nose – as she always did when she was deep in thought. Then with a sigh she went to her bag and pulled out a little bottle. "Here," she said, throwing it to Tom. "Have a swig of that. The juice will get rid of your tiredness. It neutralizes the energy lull that ghosts give you. As you've rightly said, your job is done. So we can use Hetty Hyssop's special recipes again, can't we?"

"Too right," said Tom, and took a swig. After taking just a couple of breaths, he felt the leaden tiredness melting away from him.

Hetty also drank some of the poppy-red liquid, then looked at him. "Do we really want to go home tomorrow, Tom?" she asked in a low voice.

Tom nudged the trap with his finger. "No," he finally said. "I suppose we should find out why a NEPGA appeared in this village and why the houses here are all moaning and groaning. I'd also like to know more about the mud and the musty stench – and what all the talk about the Twelfth Messenger means."

"Rather a lot of questions, isn't it?" Hetty Hyssop remarked. "And I fear they all have rather less than delightful answers."

"Maybe the NEPGA can give us some of them," said Tom – but Hetty Hyssop shook her head.

"Not in its energy-weakened state. We'd have to let it out, and that's not a particularly appealing idea. No." She looked out the window again. "We have to find out more about this village," she mused. "What on Earth's going on with all this mud? As you said, the musty smell doesn't indicate Swamp Ghosts. And anyway, the mud would be dripping from the taps or running down the walls of the houses, but here the whole ground beneath the village seems to be turning to goo. A very strange and disturbing phenomenon."

"The vicarage is so crooked, it looks as if it's already half sunk," said Tom.

Worried, Hetty Hyssop turned to him. "What did you say?"

"Well, it was crooked!" Tom repeated. "Didn't you notice?"

Hetty Hyssop shook her head. "Oh dear," she murmured. "This reminds me of something. A case in Cornwall, England. It was more than ten years ago, so I don't remember it properly, but . . ." She quickly slipped her coat back on. "I'm just going to have another look outside, Tom," she said. "I've got an awful suspicion, but I hope I'm wrong." Hastily she slung her bag over her shoulder and went to the door.

"Wait! I'm coming with you, of course!" cried Tom. "But what are we going to do with the NEPGA?"

"The trap is secure for at least another twenty-four hours," replied Hetty Hyssop, opening the door. "Curses, I just wish that silly ASG were here. We really could do with a bit of ghostly help right now."

A Bad Suspicion

"Good gracious, I'm right!" moaned Hetty Hyssop once they were standing in the dark street. Only a couple of yards from the inn door, a big muddy hole gaped through the road surface. Tom didn't remember its having been there when they returned to the inn. Frowning, Hetty Hyssop crouched next to it and sniffed. "No two ways about it," she said. "The same musty smell that's in the air, only much, much worse."

At that very moment, a gigantic dirty brown bubble formed at Tom's feet. The bubble arched higher and higher until it burst with an unsavory belch. The stinking mud splattered Tom right up to his forehead, and once he'd wiped the muddy spray off his glasses, cursing as he did so, he couldn't believe his eyes: A stone slab had pushed its way up through the mud. It loomed up out of the road like a jagged gray tooth.

"What does that mean?" whispered Tom – and

whirled around in horror. Behind him was a squelching and slurping sound, and a piece of the pavement sank.

"It means" — said Hetty Hyssop, pulling Tom a couple of steps backward as the ground beneath his feet began to gurgle like boiling chocolate pudding — "it means nothing good. If this is what I think it is, then we're dealing with something very, very old and very, very powerful. This has got nothing to do with Category Three dangers now, Tom. Do you remember what the vicar's sister said?"

Tom swallowed. "She said the village was cursed," he replied.

"Precisely." Hetty Hyssop nodded. "Now, you know what I think of such talk. But whatever it is that's stirring here has probably been making its presence felt for ages already. What did Hornheaver say?"

"That the village attracts ghosts like flies." Tom looked around uneasily. A street sign was tipping slowly into the mud.

Hetty Hyssop nodded again. "Exactly. It all fits. Come on, let's go and have another look at the church square." She quickly strode off across the muddy street. Tom stumbled along behind her.

"What all fits? And how old is very, very old?" he cried.

"Five, maybe ten thousand years old, for all I know," replied Hetty Hyssop.

Tom swallowed. The oldest ghost he'd dealt with so far had been a totally moldy Baroness, a HIGA of the most revolting type. And so far as Tom could recall, she had only been about four hundred years old. The older the ghost, according to *Basics for Ghosthunters*, the more powerful it is. *A charming prospect*, thought Tom, remembering with a good deal of unease how he had only just managed to get the better of the moldy Baroness.

"Tom!" Hetty Hyssop stopped so abruptly that Tom almost stumbled into her. "We've got to get a move on."

Something had emerged from the ground in front of Bogpool Church. Looming up from a lake of gurgling mud was a massive stone altar. A roughly cut staircase led up to it. The gray steps shimmered strangely pale under the starless night sky, while the fog swirled around the altar as if it wanted to bid it welcome with its white hands.

"When I get *my* hands on that Slimeblott . . ." spat Hetty Hyssop between clenched teeth. Tom had never seen her so angry. Suddenly she turned and marched back to the inn.

Without a moment's hesitation she went behind the reception desk and banged on the door marked PRIVATE. "Hornheaver!" she cried. "Hornheaver, wake up!"

Tom heard a faint swearing from behind the door, and then their host's sleepy face appeared. "What on Earth —" he started bellowing, but Hetty Hyssop immediately interrupted him.

"Get on the phone!" she said. "Wake the whole village! Every inhabitant! Tell them they need to pack just the essentials, then go straight to family or friends — the farther from here, the better!"

Erwin Hornheaver opened his mouth, but Hetty Hyssop didn't let him get a word in. "Tell them their lives are at risk. And anyone who doesn't believe you should just look at the church square. Off you go, get on with it!"

"What's going on in the church square?" cried Hornheaver as Hetty Hyssop and Tom dashed up the

stairs. "If it's some silly ghost — we're all used to them!"

"It's not a ghost!" Tom called down over the banister. "And put your galoshes on if you go out. Has it rained a lot here in the last few weeks?"

"No!" growled Erwin Hornheaver. "What on Earth's going on? It's the middle of the night!"

"Get on the phone!" Tom replied simply, disappearing up the stairs.

"Can you get into the **LOAG** on your computer, Tom?" asked Hetty Hyssop, locking the door with trembling fingers.

"The **L**ist **O**f **A**ll Known **G**hosts?" Tom nodded. "'Course I can."

It was dark in their room, but Hugo flickered moldy green above the bed. In his left hand, he was balancing the ball containing the NEPGA.

"Hello-elllooooo!" he breathed as Tom and Hetty Hyssop came in. "What's this cuuuuute little thiiiing yoooou've caught here?" And — *boing!* — he caught the COCOT in his other hand.

"Hugo, put that down at once!" cried Tom. "The trap releases itself if another ghost gets hold of it!"

Hugo dropped the ball as if it had burned his fingers. The trap fell onto the bed and came to rest on Tom's pillow.

"Where were you?" Hetty Hyssop snapped at the ASG whilst Tom carefully put the COCOT back into the ashtray.

"Why? I wasn't supposed to be heeeeelping!" Hugo answered defiantly. "I've been loooooooking for someone to friiiiighten. Yooooou can't stop me from dooooing that. I tickled a niiiice fat one. Oooooh, how she squeeeeealed. . . ." Hugo shook with laughter to such an extent that he banged his head against the ceiling light.

"Your haunting really doesn't interest anyone at the moment," Tom interrupted him irritably. "Haven't you figured out what's going on?"

"Why? What is iiiiit?" Curious, Hugo floated to the window and stuck his head through the glass. Then he drew it back in, smacking his lips faintly. "It's foooooggy, and there's a deliiiiicious smell of musssst and moooold."

"Forget it!" murmured Tom, opening his laptop and calling up the LOAG archive. When he typed in

63

Bogpool, the screen filled so quickly that Tom's eyes could barely follow it all. "Well, look at that lot," he murmured. "If Slimeblott didn't know anything about this, I'm an ASG."

"Read it out," said Hetty Hyssop, sitting down next to Tom on the edge of the bed. And Tom read:

BOGPOOL: small village on the edge of a swamp, now largely drained. Settlement believed to have been founded in the 6th century AD. However, archaeological discoveries in the surrounding area suggest that a pagan center of worship existed in the same place in the pre-Christian era. For the last couple of years, **Bogpool** has become known for its increasing number of ghostly presences. Reported thus far: three Danger Category One BOSGs; two FOFIFOs (Type B, wily but not life-threatening); two HIGAs of unknown vintage (possibly dating back to the pre-Christian era); one ASG; two BLAGDOs; and one WHIWHI.

One universal and unusual fact about all documented apparitions in **Bogpool**: Although the ghosts in question stubbornly resisted all attempts to drive them out, they then, for no obvious reason, inexplicably and unexpectedly disappeared, never to be seen again.

Tom lifted his head.

"Did you count them up?" asked Hetty Hyssop.

Tom nodded. "Twelve. Including our NEPGA." He typed something else on his computer keyboard. "I'll just call up the RICOG files," he said. "Perhaps they'll have something for the keyword *Twelfth Messenger....*"

"Tweeeeelfth Messenger?" Hugo recoiled in such horror that half of him disappeared into the wall.

Hetty Hyssop turned to him. "Aha, our ghostly friend is evidently not unfamiliar with this expression. Spit it out, Hugo. Where do these messengers come from? And who sends them?"

Hugo, however, raised his pale hands defensively. "Oh no. Some thiiiiiings are best not talked abooooout. Toooooo old. Toooooo powerfuuuul!"

"I've got it!" cried Tom, craning over his screen. "TWELFTH MESSENGER," he read aloud.

During the last hundred years, there have been four recorded cases of ghosthunters capturing ghosts that claimed to be the "Twelfth Messenger." In every case, a dreadful kind of ghost, the so-called Prince of Demons, or Zargoroth, appeared just a few days after the event and in the same place where the messenger ghosts were captured. Little more is known of the appearance or capabilities of this creature, but it is apparently extremely powerful. For what little information exists, see also ZARGOROTH.

The Zargoroth, in fact, announces itself via *thirteen* ghostly messengers. The initial ghostly apparitions are primarily harmless local ghosts, but the menace of the messengers increases as the appearance of their barbaric master draws nearer. Typically, Black Ghost Dogs (BLAGDOs) appear at some point. And the Twelfth Messenger is always a Negative Projection (NEPGA). Only in the last five years or so have these penultimate apparitions become relatively easy to fight, thanks to the invention of the Negative Neutralizer Belt (NENEB). The thirteenth and final messenger is irrevocably and inevitably a Ghost of Death (GHODE). **Warning:** The Ghost of Death appears more quickly if one makes the mistake of catching the Twelfth Messenger.

Tom nervously pushed up his glasses. "Oh, great," he murmured. "We've already made that mistake. What now?"

"We don't take a single step outside that door without protective goggles," replied Hetty Hyssop.

"Hohohoooo, protectiiiive goggles!" Hugo folded his arms across his chest with a grim expression. "If a Ghooooost of Death sees yoou, yooooou're dead within the hoooour."

"That's not remotely true, you conceited ghost," said Hetty Hyssop impatiently. "The goggles protect you for a good five minutes. And that's plenty of time to turn your head away."

Hugo just wrinkled up his nose. Then he bent down to Tom. "Yoooou're my friend," he breathed.

"Even iiiif yoooou *are* always sayiiiing meeeean things abooooout salt and eggs. Take yooooour NEPGA and fleeeee. His master is a bloodsuuuuucker, a devourer of huuuumans. . . ."

Tom pretended not to be impressed at all. "Oh, come on, Hugo," he said, even though what he'd read had already disconcerted him somewhat. "We've seen off IRGs and GILIGs. Why not this Zargoroth? Someone ought to put a stop to him."

"Put a stoooooop to him?" cried Hugo, irritated. "Dooooo yooooon know what he gets up toooo? He'll gobble yoooou up, riiiip yoooooou to shreds in the air, suuuuuck the —"

"Tom," Hetty Hyssop interrupted him. "Just type in *Zargoroth*, would you?"

Tom did as she asked, although his fingers were trembling. While the computer was trawling through the RICOG files, Tom looked at his watch. It was two in the morning. The night was by no means over. . . .

ZARGOROTH also Prince of Demons; The One Who Arises From The Mud: minimal information available, as nobody has ever encountered this demon without losing his life or his sanity. All that's known for sure is that the Zargoroth is attracted to old pagan centers of worship – which leads some experts to conclude that they are dealing with a Nature Ghost (NAG) of human origin. This theory, however, is disputed.

During the last century the destruction of several villages has been attributed to a Zargoroth. Thus far, four colleagues, all very successful and highly experienced ghosthunters, have attempted to take on the apparition. Two were attacked by Black Ghost Dogs and never seen again. The other two looked the Thirteenth Messenger – always a Ghost of Death – in the face, and died within the hour. There is as yet, therefore, no empirical information regarding the appearance and powers of the Zargoroth. All that exists are pictures of the devastation the demon wreaks – and one tiny clue: namely, that all clocks start to move backward approximately half an hour before the beast appears. Click <u>here</u> for the pictures.

"Good gracious!" moaned Hetty Hyssop. A rather fuzzy black-and-white photo appeared on the screen. There was not much more to be seen than a massive heap of mud. A solitary church steeple stuck out of it along with a couple of upended trees and a stone altar.

"What did Hornheaver say when we arrived?" asked Hetty Hyssop, as Tom clicked for the next image. "That he'd sent twelve messages to ROGA, wasn't it?"

Tom nodded. The second picture was no better.

"Twelve – I ask you!" Hetty Hyssop stamped her foot so angrily that Hugo wobbled off the bed in horror. "Lotan Slimeblott knew what was going to happen to us here, Tom. I'd bet my entire ghosthunting arsenal on it. Oh, that vengeful, sly, incompetent, brain-dead . . ." She gasped for breath. She'd run out of insults.

"We'll show that villain," said Tom. "Just think how annoyed he'll be if we take on this Zargoroth! But we'd better keep an eye on our watches from now on."

There was a knock at the door. Erwin Hornheaver stuck his fat head into the room.

"I've called 'em all," he growled. "They didn't want to go, but they've all gathered in the school so that you can tell them a bit about the altar and why their houses are being scrunched."

Hetty Hyssop stood up with a deep sigh. "Come on, Tom," she said. "It'll use up valuable time, but . . ."

"Stop! I could dooooo it!" breathed Hugo, wobbling out from behind the door with an evil smile. "What do yoooooou think?" he asked, poking their landlord in the chest with an icy finger.

"Stop it, Hugo!" cried Tom, irritated, but the sight of a moldy green ASG didn't seem to faze Hornheaver in the least.

"We had one like him here before," he said, looking Hugo up and down so contemptuously that the

ASG immediately shrank half a foot. "These moldy-noses don't like salt, so I discovered."

"They don't like raw eggs, either," Tom added, pushing past Hugo. "You could make yourself useful for a change," he said as he passed the ASG, who was still gazing at the fearless innkeeper, totally flabbergasted. "Find out if this Thirteenth Messenger is already on the loose."

"Oooooh, so yoooou're asking meeeee for help all of a sudden?" Hugo cried indignantly after Tom, who was already running down the stairs. "What about a nice little 'Pleeeeeaaase, Huuuuugo'?"

"Please, Hugo!" cried Tom. Then he followed Hetty Hyssop and Erwin Hornheaver out into the foggy night.

A Daring Plan

It took Hetty Hyssop and Tom nearly a quarter of an hour to convince the inhabitants of Bogpool that their village had turned into one of the most dangerous places on Earth. Packed together like sardines, most of them still in bathrobes and pajamas, the villagers sat listening, their faces ashen with horror, to Tom's description of the Zargoroth. Only the vicar's sister interrupted Tom several times to call out that she'd said so all along. When Hetty Hyssop told them how deadly the Thirteenth Messenger was, switching the lights off as she ended her speech, there was no way the Bogpoolers were staying in their seats any longer.

Ten minutes later, Tom, Hetty Hyssop, and Erwin Hornheaver were standing alone in the dark hall, surrounded by nothing but overturned chairs and lost bedroom slippers.

"Well, Hornheaver," said Hetty Hyssop. "Pack whatever you want to save from the mud and get yourself to safety."

But Erwin Hornheaver didn't stir. He stared blackly at the gurgling mud that was flowing through the open front door from the playground. "And what are you two going to do now, may I ask?"

"Well, we'll try to prepare a nice welcome for the Zargoroth," replied Tom.

Erwin Hornheaver nodded and surveyed the upturned chairs. "Reckon you two could use a bit of help, couldn't you?"

Tom and Hetty Hyssop exchanged surprised looks.

"Y'know," Hornheaver continued, "I've never been very afraid of these ghosts. I was a boxer once upon a time, before I inherited my aunt's inn, and I only give up if I'm knocked out. If you get my drift."

"That really is a very generous offer, Hornheaver," said Hetty Hyssop. "And I hope you've got some idea of what you're getting yourself into. Tom, have we got a third pair of protective goggles with us?"

Tom rummaged around in his backpack. "I haven't got any on me," he said finally. "But I think there's a spare in the suitcase."

"Good." Hetty Hyssop nodded and gave Erwin Hornheaver an appreciative thump on the shoulders. "It's not often that someone offers to help us," she said. "And tonight's a night when we'd really appreciate it, isn't it, Tom?"

"Too right," murmured Tom, who was disconcerted to see that the mud was flowing faster and faster into the school.

It was now twenty to three. Dawn was still hours away. And they didn't have the faintest idea how they were going to fight whatever was coming for them.

By twenty after three, Bogpool was a deserted village. Erwin Hornheaver had walked around the place and hadn't encountered a single living being. Not even a cat or a hen. The Bogpoolers had taken their livestock and horses with them. And mud and fog were taking possession of one house after another.

"Good!" said Hetty Hyssop, pacing energetically up and down their room. "Everyone's gone, so we can get to work. How are you getting on, Tom?"

"Still nothing," Tom spat through clenched teeth. Ever since they'd gotten back from the assembly hall, he'd been crouching in front of the computer, typing in one keyword after another – in the desperate hope of turning up some clue as to how they were supposed to fight the Zargoroth. Tom's eyes hurt, and he had to keep taking off his glasses to rub away the veil of tiredness that made the words on the screen swim around in front of him. "Nothing," he said again, and shook his head. "We just don't know enough about this ghost. It's enough to drive you crazy."

"That NEPGA isn't talking, eeeeeeeeeeither!" breathed Hugo, tapping the COCOT with his finger. "Iiiii've triiiiiied reeeeeeeally hard toooooo persuaaaaaade him, ghoooooost to ghoooooost, but Iiiii can't get a peeeeeep ooout of him. Conceeeeeited frazzled idiiiiiiiot ghoooost!"

Tom sat bolt upright.

"What?" Both Hugo and Hetty Hyssop looked at him.

"That's it!" Tom cried, snapping the computer shut. "That's our only chance!"

"Does he often speak in riddles?" growled Hornheaver, giving Hetty Hyssop a mug of hot coffee and Tom his fourth can of soda.

"Hugo, put the COCOT under my pillow," said Tom, "so the NEPGA can't hear what we're talking about."

The ASG did as he was told, and Tom lowered his voice.

"There's only one thing to do!" he whispered. "We let the NEPGA go, then follow it to its master. Once we've actually set eyes on the Zargoroth, we might be able to identify what kind of ghost that is — and how we can fight it!"

Tom felt really pleased with himself and his idea, but Hetty Hyssop frowned. "That's a dangerous idea, my dear boy," she said. "Even if I were to agree to such a plan, how do you propose to follow a NEPGA? Human legs are definitely too slow, and what are you going to do if it flies? Or if it just floats through a wall?"

"We could coat it in a mixture of baking powder and scouring sand," replied Tom. "That slows ghosts down and stops them from going through walls. And as far as flying is concerned, you know I'm really not that keen on it, but . . ." He turned to Hugo and didn't finish his sentence.

The ASG turned the color of pale mold. "Ooooooh! What's that looooook suuuuupposed to meeeeeean?"

"You can carry me on your back!" said Tom. "In all that fog out there, you're as good as invisible, but you can see the NEPGA as clearly as anything. We can follow it to its master, find out exactly what we're dealing with — and then fly back here. Not very difficult, is it?"

"Ha! Ha-haaaaa!" Hugo rolled his garish green eyes. "Not veeery difficult, heeeeee says!"

"You ought to let Hugo do it on his own, Tom," said Hetty Hyssop. "The job isn't half as dangerous for a ghost as it is for a human."

"Pah, it's dangerous eeeeenooooough!" grumbled Hugo — but Hetty Hyssop gave him such a fierce look that he shut up.

"He can't do it on his own!" cried Tom. "He doesn't know anything about identifying and classifying ghosts. I bet Hugo can recognize at most five percent of them!"

"At mosssssst!" breathed Hugo, showing his agreement by smacking Tom on the back.

Hetty Hyssop shook her head. "I don't like this," she said. "No. There has to be another way. After all, the Ghost of Death's spooking around out there as well."

"Oh, I've got the protective goggles," said Tom dismissively. "That really isn't a problem."

Erwin Hornheaver hadn't spoken thus far.

But now he cleared his throat. "Leave the boy alone!" he told Hetty Hyssop, topping up her coffee mug. "He can do it. You told me yourself what a first-class ghost-hunter he is."

Tom was thankful for this unexpected support, but Hetty Hyssop looked at him and sighed. "Well, yes, he certainly is!" she said. "He's one of the best, one of the very best."

Tom turned as red as tomato juice.

"That settles it, then," he said, self-consciously setting his glasses straight. "Have you got any baking powder and scouring sand, Mr. Hornheaver?"

"Erwin," growled Erwin Hornheaver. "My name is Erwin, lad, and I think I've got both."

This was Tom's plan: Hugo was to play with the COCOT until the trap – oops, what a shame! – released itself, whereupon he was to throw it out the window in horror. There, Tom would already be waiting with a full sprinkler and would bombard the NEPGA with baking powder and scouring sand as soon as it freed itself from the trap.

"I just hope Hugo doesn't mess it all up!" whispered Tom as he and Hetty Hyssop stood below in the foggy street. The white haze was so thick by now that Tom could hardly make out their bedroom window. He himself was barely visible, either. He was wearing what's known in ghosthunting circles as a **GHOSID** (**GHO**st-**SI**mulation **D**isguise): pale, moldy green overalls with a hood and gloves of the same color; and his face was covered in almost a pound of makeup that went by the name of "Ghostly Pallor." On top of that, he was surrounded by a faint smell of cellars, as the smaller, harmless ghosts often are. Tom, unfortunately, hadn't been able to change anything about his body temperature, but it was entirely possible for some ghosts to radiate something very similar to human warmth.

There was just one more problem, and it worried Hetty Hyssop more than anything else: Tom needed to wear the goggles to protect himself from being looked at by the Ghost of Death — but he was supposed to be disguised as a ghost, and no real ghost would wear such a thing. Tom, however, promised to have them always on hand and to put them on as soon as he and Hugo were on their way back. Thankfully, his normal glasses wouldn't give him away.

Wearing glasses is not unusual in the ghostly world.

Tom pulled the moldy green hood down even more tightly over his forehead. The village, devoid of humans, was ghostly silent; only the stones were still moaning and the mud gurgling – and Hugo's voice resounded clearly down to them through the milky darkness.

"Soooooo, it's maaaaaaking yoooooou dizzzzzy, yooooooooou shaaaaady character, is it?" Tom could hear him howling. "Cooooooome on. What's it liiiiiiike in there, my liiiiittle goooooooldfish?"

"Ten more seconds," whispered Hetty Hyssop, not taking her eyes off her illuminated wristwatch. "Nine, eight, seven . . ."

"Yoooooou'll loooooook great in the muuuuuuu-seum for captuuuuured ghoooooosts!" breathed Hugo. "A reeeeeal jewel in oooooour coooooollection."

"Three!" whispered Hetty Hyssop. "Two, one, and – zero!"

Holding their breath, they looked up at the fog-shrouded window. "Come on, Hugo!" whispered Tom, holding the full sprinkler. At that very moment, it happened.

The COCOT flew through the air . . . and landed in a lake of mud.

"Curses!" hissed Tom. "It's sinking. What now?"

But the NEPGA was already arising from the mud. Dripping, it raised itself from the swamp like the shadow of a dark dream.

This was Tom's moment. With one leap, he bounded into the street, sank up to his knees in the brown goo — and raised the sprinkler.

"Yoooooou!" breathed the NEPGA, floating threateningly over to him. "Yoooooooou dared . . ."

"Not one foot farther!" cried Tom, sprinkling Erwin Hornheaver's entire supply of baking powder and scouring sand onto its dark body. The NEPGA coughed and tried with smoky gray fingers to wipe the burning powder off, but it was completely coated. With an angry screech, the ghost flew up into the sky — and disappeared into the swirling fog.

"Hugo, where are you?" cried Tom.

The ASG was barely visible in the fog. With icy fingers, he lifted Tom up onto his shoulders.

"Remember the Thirteenth Messenger, Tom," cried Hetty Hyssop, "and don't, whatever you do, try to fight the Zargoroth on your own!"

But Tom and Hugo had already been swallowed up by the fog.

The Ghosts' Cave

At first, Tom thought the NEPGA had escaped too quickly. It was nowhere to be seen; the fog wrapped them with stinking clouds. They blinded Tom and made it almost impossible to breathe. But then, all of a sudden, the dark figure of the fleeing ghost appeared out of the mist, right in front of them. It was flying as slowly as Tom had hoped, the baking powder and scouring sands acting like lead weights on its limbs. Above the church square the NEPGA lost altitude, and Tom thought for a moment that it was going to disappear back into the church. However, the ghost flew on, past the church steeple, over the vicarage roof, on and on, until the houses of Bogpool were all behind it.

"Where's it going?" Tom whispered to Hugo. "Do you recognize anything?"

"Nothing!" replied Hugo, slowing down in line with the NEPGA. It seemed almost to be floating on the spot, like a starless hole in the cloudy night. Then it suddenly dropped to Earth like a stone.

"After it, Hugo!" Tom cried in a muffled voice. "Quickly! Or we'll lose it!"

Hugo dropped down. A swampy meadow appeared out of the fog. Tom slipped off Hugo's shoulders and sank up to his knees in the damp, pale yellow grass. He looked around. There was no sign of the NEPGA. Its dark figure had vanished as if it had simply dissolved. But a few feet away, gigantic stones loomed up from the grass. Each of them was at least twelve feet high.

"Standing stones," murmured Tom. "Hetty was right: We really are dealing with something seriously ancient."

The stones formed a circle, as far as Tom could tell. "Looks like a pagan shrine or something," he whispered to Hugo. "Come on, let's go and take a closer look."

Hesitantly the ASG floated behind him. "This smells like a real ghooooosts' nest if yooooou ask meeeee," he breathed. "Daaaark ghosts, paaaale ghosts, liiiitle ones, biiiig ones, they're all here."

Tom sighed. "Just as we feared," he murmured. "Come on, let's get it over with."

The fog swirled like smoke from between the stones, and Tom could barely heave his boots out of the swamp. "Looks as if all the trouble's been coming from here," he whispered. "Be thankful you can fly, Hugo. If this keeps on, I'll be up to my neck in . . ."

He got no further. Hugo pressed his cold fingers against his mouth and pulled him to his chest. Two black dogs as big as calves had appeared between the stones. Their red eyes glowed like fire. They looked

around inquisitively, panting and showing their long pale teeth – then disappeared into the night.

Tom started breathing again only when Hugo put him back on his feet.

"Ghoooost Dogs!" whispered the ASG. "Stuuuupid creeeeatures. All it takes is a bit of ASG odor, and they don't smell the little people creeeeeping up tooooo their maaaaster's house!"

"Well, thank goodness for that!" murmured Tom, taking six deep breaths. This slowed down his heart rate, although it didn't have any effect on his wobbly knees. "Right!" he whispered, trying to sound calm. "Now at least we know where our gray friend disappeared to. Shall I . . . go first?"

"Very brave!" mocked Hugo and pushed him behind his back. "But I think yoooou'll be a biiiit more conspiiiicuuuous in this fog than I will be – despite yooooour hilaaaaariiiioous ghostly garb. So yooou stay behind me, OK?"

Tom nodded. He had to admit that he was glad to accept Hugo's offer. Silently he pulled an **A**ir **C**harger out of his backpack. The thing generated air vibrations that caused ghosts to tremble violently but was small enough to be hidden up his sleeve. The tiny thing had more than once helped Tom to keep all sorts of spectral opponents off his back for at least a couple of valuable seconds.

Hugo had already disappeared between the stones. Holding his breath, Tom followed him. The ground squelched with every step he took, as if it wanted to betray him. Above them, the moon appeared through the fog. It was floating in a pool of rusty red light, and the huge stones threw spooky shadows onto the place where they were standing.

"Hey, look at that!" whispered Tom, grabbing Hugo's arm.

In the middle of the stone circle, a large square chasm yawned in the mud. Fog billowed out of it like smoke. It made Tom's eyes water and almost took his breath away. Holding his sleeve across his mouth, he cautiously stepped over to the edge of the abyss. A staircase made of roughly carved stone descended steeply into the depths. After a few steps, it disappeared into the grubby white mist and pitch-black darkness.

"Let the fuuun begin!" Hugo breathed in Tom's ear, and floated down the staircase, flickering. Tom followed him, trying to ignore his heart pounding in his throat. He hated being underground, but it was an unfortunate occupational hazard of ghosthunting. The steps went farther and farther down. The air was becoming ever more stale, until Tom felt it was as difficult to breathe as if an elephant were sitting on his chest. In the pale yellow light that Hugo emitted (ASGs make excellent flashlights when it's dark), Tom could see that the walls on either side of the steps were carved with letters. He'd never been particularly good at history, but if he wasn't much mistaken, these letters were called runes − if in fact they were letters at all. There were also pictures of gigantic bulls, painted in brown on the stone. Or maybe it wasn't paint, but . . . ?

Tom preferred not to follow that train of thought.

All of a sudden, a noise echoed up to them from the depths. It sounded like the roar of a savage beast. Tom pressed his hands against the cold stone and stood still. *Come on, don't panic. Take six deep breaths!* he thought. *Of course you'll get out of here alive. No two ways about it.* At that moment Hugo turned to him, put his finger to his ghostly lips, and waved.

They had reached the bottom of the stairs. Rusty red light came through a door in the stony wall, and as Tom peeped under Hugo's arm, he saw something that would probably have made a more inexperienced ghosthunter drop dead on the spot. . . .

A wide staircase led down into a vast cave. It was filled with a haze of vile-stinking mist, and through the mist Tom spotted ghostly apparitions of all kinds: musty BOSGs, HIGAs with dented helmets and bloodshot eyes, several smaller STKNOGs (who were probably responsible for the revolting stink), three White Ladies, a huge rusty-red RattleR. . . . Oh, it was impossible to tell them apart, never mind count them. They were all swirling and floating around a massive block of stone that loomed up in the middle of the cave like a throne. Directly in front of it – Tom could see it quite clearly – floated the NEPGA, whose dark form was still disfigured by baking powder and scouring sand. But Tom barely wasted any time looking at him. He only had eyes for what was crouching high on top of the stone block.

At first he couldn't see the ominous figure clearly, for two Ghost Dogs were floating around it, panting. But then their master bellowed hoarsely to shoo them away – and Tom saw who they were dealing with.

One look was enough. "By all the planets!" he murmured, and shuddered.

The Zargoroth shook his massive head and sniffed. He had the head of a giant bull. His huge horns shimmered as pale as moonlight. From the shoulders downward, though, the demon had a human form, apart from the fact that his clawed feet were covered in rusty-red fur.

A minotaurean demon! Tom thought, his heart beating so violently that it seemed like his ribs would crack. *So much for those beasts being long since extinct!*

The Zargoroth's eyes were black pools, abyssal and filled with hatred. Bellowing angrily, he turned back to the NEPGA. It was the same bellowing Tom had heard on the steps.

The NEPGA cowered and wrung its dark hands. Tom quickly pulled his **G**host-**S**peak **I**nterpreter out of his pocket. Hetty Hyssop had invented it herself; it was barely any bigger than a cork. Although it was questionable whether it would work with the Zargoroth, Tom wanted at least to try. But just as he was about to shove the little silvery gray thing into his ear, something pushed him from behind. Tom whirled around and stared straight at the dripping chest of a

Swamp Ghost. Quickly, he shook the Air Charger out of his sleeve, but the BOSG just pushed Tom and Hugo impatiently down the stairs and then floated past them to the Zargoroth's throne.

Tom looked around uneasily. Now he was right in the middle of the ghostly crowd. Hugo had maneuvered behind him. The ASG seemed to like the crush. Tom saw him looking around for the White Ladies. But Tom was living in terror of the moment when one of the ghosts would get a whiff of his human smell or be surprised by his warm breath. Then he'd be a goner.

He tried again to push the Ghost-Speak Interpreter into his ear, and this time he managed it. As Tom had feared, the contraption didn't work very well with the Zargoroth, but he could make out a few words amidst the general clamor.

"Before dawn," Tom thought he heard. "The altar . . . all mine . . ." And then: " . . . Thirteenth Messenger already back?" Tom looked around in horror – remembering just at that moment that it wasn't exactly wise to look at a Ghost of Death. The Zargoroth was grunting on, but however desperately Tom turned and pressed it, the interpreter didn't decipher a single word more. Tom surreptitiously pushed back a glove and looked at his watch. It was still going clockwise, although it seemed as if the hands were moving forward too slowly.

Tom jabbed his arm into Hugo's pale side. "Come on!" he whispered. "Let's go. We've seen enough."

"D'yoooou thiiiink?" breathed Hugo, looking at a White Lady who smelled so strongly of jasmine, it made Tom feel faint.

"Yes, I do!" he hissed, grabbing Hugo's arm impatiently and making his way through the crowd.

They had no time to lose. The GHOSID wouldn't last forever. The scents were becoming less and less effective by the minute, and Tom had the unpleasant feeling that most of the makeup had already come off his face. A STKNOG turned around, a wary look on its face, as Tom forced his way under its arm, and one of the Ghost Dogs that had been floating around the Zargoroth's throne sniffed as if its black nose had picked up something suspicious.

"The scent!" Tom burst out as he and Hugo sped back to the staircase. "I don't think it's working anymore. We've got to get out of here. Quickly."

Before he knew what was happening, Hugo had

clasped him under his arm and was floating up the steps with him.

The steps leading upward seemed even longer to Tom than they had on the way down. He could hardly wait to tell Hetty Hyssop what he had found out — so much that he had almost forgotten to be afraid.

"It's a minotaur, Hugo!" he burst out as soon as Hugo was floating outside in the fresh air. "I'd never have guessed there were still any of these monsters

96

around. Pretty dangerous creatures, definitely, but not invincible – oh no!"

"Oh nooooo?" breathed Hugo, lifting him onto his back and looking anxiously around. But nothing stirred in the stone circle. The moon still swam in a red light above them, and the shadows of the stones reached for them like black fingers. The ASG raised himself up into the air, as pale as mist. As they left the stone circle behind, a shudder suddenly ran across Tom. An indeterminate fear overwhelmed him, as if something dreadful were awaiting him in the darkness.

Oh, nonsense! Nothing but a typical reaction to ghosts, he thought, pinching both earlobes tightly. This normally put an end to such moods.

"A real minotaur!" he said, bending right down over Hugo's shoulder. "A hideous sight, you have to admit it. But we've got a chance, Hugo! At least now we know what we're dealing with! Can't you float any faster? I suspect he'll take possession of the village before dawn!"

"Noooo, I can't goooo any faaaaaster!" Hugo breathed irritably. He flew higher and higher, until the fog was left way beneath them. "I really dooooon't know what yooooou're so pleased about! These demons are a barbaric buuuunch! They rip their victims up in the aaaair like torn-up sheets, and they're partiiiicularly fond of bloooood!"

"Yeah, yeah, I know." Tom took a deep breath. It felt good to get some fresh air into his lungs again after all the fog and musty fug. "That blood stuff is pretty hideous, true, but they're not that clever. What's more, they're terrified of fire. And there's a sixteenth-century account of minotaurean demons . . ."

"Sixteenth ceeeentury, well, well!" breathed Hugo mockingly. "Rather a looooong time ago, by my reckoning. And whaaaat does it say?"

The spire of Bogpool Church appeared beneath them, and Hugo slowly started to descend.

"I don't exactly know, but I can find out!" Tom replied impatiently and took off his glasses. They were completely covered in ghostly makeup. "In any case, someone did once defeat one of these demons, and if it can happen once . . ."

Tom didn't finish his sentence. For at that moment, it happened.

Something pale and shapeless emerged from the veil of mist beneath them. Black eyes stared straight at

Tom, who was still shortsightedly polishing his glasses.

"Watch ooooout!" cried Hugo. But it was already too late. Tom lifted his head — and looked straight into the eyes of the Thirteenth Messenger.

The messenger emitted a gentle moan, twisted its pale mouth into a smile that chilled Tom's heart, and floated through him and Hugo like a wind that was made of nothing but ice.

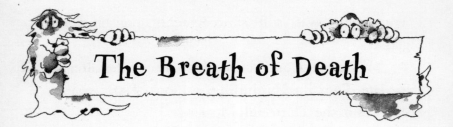

The Breath of Death

Hetty Hyssop was still leaning by the inn door when Hugo returned with Tom. Erwin Hornheaver had tried several times to persuade her to wait inside. Hetty, however, had remained outside, even though the mud was already swirling around her ankles.

"For goodness' sake, Tom!" she cried. "Why do you think you've got a walkie-talkie in your backpack? I've died at least twenty-three times because I didn't hear anything from you."

"Sorry," murmured Tom, climbing off Hugo's back. "I completely forgot about it."

"My gracious, you look terrible!" said Hetty Hyssop, looking anxiously into his face. "I hope it's just because of your GHOSID. Don't keep me on tenterhooks any longer. What happened? Did you see the Zargoroth?"

Tom set his glasses straight. "Yes . . ." he said weakly. "You could say we have good and bad news."

Hugo pressed his icy fingers to his face and uttered a faint wail. Hetty Hyssop looked at him anxiously.

"It's a minotaurean demon," said Tom, rubbing his eyes. They were hurting horribly. "He's got an entire army of Second and Third Category ghosts gathered around him and, if we can trust your interpreting device, he'll be here before daybreak."

Hetty Hyssop frowned. "A minotaur? Good gracious. I thought they'd died out at least four hundred years ago. Was that the good news or the bad?"

"The good," replied Tom. "The bad news is . . ."

Hugo began to wail as if the sky were raining salt.

"What happened?" asked Hetty Hyssop. "For pity's sake, Hugo, be quiet!"

"We met the Thirteenth Messenger," replied Tom. "And I looked at him. Without protective goggles."

Hetty Hyssop turned as pale as an ASG. "By all gods and devils, Tom!" she burst out. Then she leaned against the wall of the inn and pressed her hands to her face.

"Oh well . . ." Tom could feel his knees beginning to tremble. "There's nothing we can do. I figure I" — his voice almost failed him — "I've got about three-quarters of an hour to live."

Hetty Hyssop stood up with a violent jerk.

"Nonsense!" she said, shaking her head vigorously. "Nonsense, I'll think of something. But we've no time to lose. How are you feeling? Are you seeing flashes of light? Are your knees already trembling?"

"It's still bearable," replied Tom. He really was making the greatest possible effort to sound brave and fearless. However, he had the unpleasant sensation that his arms and legs were slowly turning to ice. And that his heart was already beating rather more slowly.

"Hugo!" commanded Hetty Hyssop. "Put Tom to bed. And don't take your eyes off him. I'll be back soon."

Before Tom could protest, Hugo had already picked him up.

"Don't go to too much bother. There's no antidote to being looked at by a Ghost of Death!" Tom murmured faintly as the ASG floated into the house with him.

"Oh yes there is!" Hetty Hyssop called after him. And she added so quietly that Tom couldn't hear it: "I've just never tried it out."

Erwin Hornheaver was standing in the kitchen warming up some canned soup for himself and the ghosthunters when Hetty Hyssop came rushing in.

"If I didn't know that such things didn't bother you," he said when he saw her ashen face, "I'd say you'd seen a ghost!"

"You've got to help me, Hornheaver," said Hetty Hyssop. "I need pine oil, marsh clover, and red food coloring. And then I need a lamp with a red lightbulb, preferably several, and the most powerful vacuum cleaner you can lay your hands on."

Erwin Hornheaver dropped his spoon in the soup and turned off the stove. "Is something wrong with the lad?" he asked.

Hetty Hyssop nodded and wiped a tear from the corner of her eye.

"The vacuum cleaner's over there in the cupboard," said Erwin Hornheaver. "That thing'd suck an elephant up off the carpet. I've not got any red lights, but I'll find some. The food coloring might be more of a problem, but there's paint over at the school, nontoxic, I think. Would that do?"

Hetty Hyssop nodded. "If need be," she said. She passed her hand across her forehead with a sigh.

Erwin Hornheaver was already standing at the door. "Don't you worry," he growled. "We'll get the lad sorted. I've got a feeling he'll be chasing plenty more ghosts in the future."

"Thank you, Hornheaver," said Hetty Hyssop, looking out through the kitchen window and into the fog. "But I'll tell you one thing: If anything happens to that boy, I'll single-handedly turn the person who landed us here into a ghost. Or my name's not Hetty Hyssop!"

Tom felt like a lump of ice, even though Hugo had covered him with everything he could find. The ASG had even torn down the curtains from the window so that he could wrap Tom up in them. But Tom was freezing. His teeth chattered, and he trembled so violently that the bed creaked. "H–H–Hugo?" he asked. (Gentle reader: Talking isn't easy when your teeth are chattering.) "Hey, is being a ghost always this cold?"

"Oh, yooooou know," breathed Hugo, looking anxiously into his icy white face. "Yooooooou soooooon get uuuused to the cold."

"Really?" murmured Tom, staring at the ceiling, where one flash of light was chasing the next. As soon as the flashes turned green, he'd once read, you had about seven minutes to live. They were lemon yellow at the moment.

Tom heard the door opening and someone coming in, but he was too weak to raise his head.

"Out, Hugo!" he heard Hetty Hyssop saying. "It could get pretty dangerous for you in here." Then she came to Tom's bed and looked down at him, concerned. "My dear Tom," she said. "You look like a **FOFUG**. How are you feeling?"

(Dear reader: FOFUG = **FO**ggy **FU**g-**G**host.)

"Icy c–c–cold!" murmured Tom, trying to clench his teeth, but they kept on chattering.

"Hurry! We've got to hurry!" he heard Hetty Hyssop saying anxiously. "Put the bowl just there, Hornheaver."

Tom managed to turn his head slightly to the right – and looked straight into a red light. The whole room was suddenly bathed in red. And at least the lamp by his bed warmed the tip of his nose ever so slightly.

"Tom, this is going to taste revolting," said Hetty Hyssop, holding a glass of bloodred liquid to his icy lips.

"What is it?" croaked Tom.

"Believe me, you don't want to know," replied Hetty Hyssop with a little smile. "Just trust me and drink it, OK?"

Tom did as he was told. He had never drunk anything so disgusting in his entire life. The red brew that Hetty Hyssop mercilessly poured into him seemed to turn into liquid fire in his body. Tom felt as if he were simultaneously freezing and burning up – a truly unpleasant sensation. But after he'd forced down the tenth sip, his teeth were no longer chattering, and a delightful warmth was spreading across his face and chest. The flashes on the ceiling had turned dark yellow, but they weren't green yet.

"Hornheaver, look!" whispered Hetty Hyssop. "I do believe it's working. When he's emptied this glass, it's your turn."

Tom forced the last three mouthfuls down, wondering what Erwin Hornheaver's turn would be, when the huge innkeeper stepped toward the bed and lifted him up.

"Ready. Steady. Go!" cried Hetty Hyssop, switching on an earsplittingly loud vacuum cleaner and holding it menacingly close to Tom's right ear. But before he had a chance to be surprised or to wonder what was going on, Erwin Hornheaver squeezed. He squeezed Tom's chest so tightly that he struggled for breath like a tadpole in the open air.

"Aaaaaaaarrrgh!" he croaked. "What's going on?"

But Hornheaver was squeezing again.

"It's coming!" cried Hetty Hyssop. "Fantastic, Hornheaver. Squeeze again!"

Tom felt as if his eyes were popping out of his head, and his ribs creaked as if they were made of rotten wood, so firmly did Hornheaver have his arms around

his body. Then Tom suddenly saw grayish-white clouds of smoke floating past his eyes.

"Yes! Brilliant!" cried Hetty, almost sucking off one of his ears with her vacuum hose. Amidst all the commotion, Tom thought he could hear a moan, a deep, muffled moan — and then he suddenly felt warm. As if fresh blood were flowing through his veins.

Erwin Hornheaver loosened his grasp somewhat and looked Tom curiously in the face.

"Oh my goodness, oh my goodness!" murmured Tom, gasping for breath. Then he blinked up at the ceiling. The flashes had disappeared. And he no longer felt like a frozen rubber doll, either.

"I guess you can put me down now!" he said to Erwin Hornheaver in a weak voice.

"If you think so!" growled the innkeeper, carefully setting Tom back on his feet. But Hetty Hyssop immediately pulled him toward the bed and sat him down.

"Look at me!" she said, shining a little red lamp into his eyes and then into his ears. Then she pulled a round mirror out of her bag and held it up in front of Tom's mouth. "Breathe in and out three times," she ordered.

Tom did as she said. The mirror misted up, as did his glasses.

"Hmm, still a bit gray," said Hetty Hyssop, "but I don't think that matters."

"What's gooooing ooooon? Can I come iiiin yet?" Hugo called through the door.

"Just one more minute!" Hetty Hyssop called back. "Hornheaver," she said as she felt Tom's pulse and shone her little light into his ears once more, "would you mind opening the window and turning off the lights, or else our ASG friend will feel anything but well in this room."

"Will do," said Erwin Hornheaver. "Well, blow me down!" he growled as he stomped to the window. "That was the craziest thing I've ever seen. Steam poured out of the lad's ears like it pours out of my kettle."

"Did it really?" asked Tom, cleaning his glasses. His fingers were already working pretty well, although they still felt as if they were made of jelly.

"Too right it did," said Hetty Hyssop, opening the door. "Hugo, come on in."

"Heeee's piiiink again!" howled Hugo, rushing across to Tom so violently that Tom dropped his glasses. "Ooooooooh!" howled Hugo, running his icy fingers through Tom's hair until it stood up like a porcupine's quills. "Ooooooooh, he's all well and waaaarm again. Yesssss!"

"But I won't be for long if you keep squeezing me like that," gasped Tom, trying to escape from Hugo's embrace. The ASG reluctantly let him go, fished Tom's glasses back up from the carpet, and put them back on his nose. Then he gave him a gentle thump on the chest.

"Oooooh, I reeeeeally thooought yooooou'd had it. I'd eeeeeven started wooooondering what kind of ghoooost yooooou miiiiight make," he breathed.

"How sweet of you," said Tom, touched, straightening his glasses. "To be honest, I also thought I was going to switch over to the ghostly side tonight." He looked inquiringly at Hetty Hyssop: "What . . . ?"

"What saved you?" she ended his sentence and smiled. "Well, a couple of potent plants that Mr. Hornheaver found at the village pharmacy, fortunately enough, mixed with a few other ingredients, fifteen red lamps — that's how many we could dig up in the village — an extra-powerful vacuum cleaner, and not least" — she threw Erwin Hornheaver a grateful look — "the considerable strength of our highly respected and most helpful host. I believe he actually did manage to squeeze the last poisonous remains of the deathly breath out of you."

Tom felt his chest, which still hurt, and managed another feeble grin. "At least now I know how it feels to be in a vise," he said.

"Sorry," growled Erwin Hornheaver. "Hope I didn't break any of your ribs."

"I don't think so," replied Tom, although he wasn't entirely sure.

"Well, then." Hetty Hyssop looked at her watch. "Quarter past four. Still a couple of hours until sunrise. Tom!" She sat down next to him on the edge of the bed with a serious expression. "You know we've never run away from a ghost before, but there's always a first time. Things being as they are, I think we should pack our bags and go. There's no way you can take on a minotaurean demon in the weakened state you're in!"

"Of course I can!" replied Tom indignantly. "I'm as good as new. Word of honor!"

"Tom!" said Hetty Hyssop sternly. "This demon is Danger Category Eight. I don't have to tell you what that means: Unpredictable. Life-threatening. Any human who confronts him stands about two-tenths of a percent chance of survival. You simply can't take on such a dangerous opponent tonight. Just be glad and grateful that you survived your encounter with his Thirteenth Messenger!"

"I am," said Tom defiantly. "But I'm not going home and leaving this bull-headed beast to destroy one village after another. It's completely out of the question. And anyway, he sent a Ghost of Death — and I take offense at that! Now, there's a sixteenth-century account of a minotaurean demon in France. . . ." Tom stood up shakily and staggered to his computer.

"Don't bother with the computer," said Hetty Hyssop and sighed. "I know the account you're talking about. Most people think it's a fairy tale, but I imagine it's based on a real event. Back then, a demon-hunter was supposed to have succeeded in destroying a minotaur that had already depopulated three villages. But the method the hunter used to achieve it was pretty risky. Not to mention that, if we were going to try it, we'd need something we'd never get ahold of in Bogpool. . . ."

"What?" asked Tom.

"A sword."

For a moment, Tom was rendered speechless. "A . . . a . . . a sword?" he stammered. "What on Earth for?"

Erwin Hornheaver cleared his throat. "There was a sword here once," he growled. "Old Benno Cherrycorn found one when he was plowing over by the forest. Three museums wanted to buy it off him, but he hung the sword above his sofa. He died last year and the thing gave his wife the creeps, so she stored it up in the attic. It might still be there."

"I don't liiiiike swooooords, eeeeither," breathed Hugo, flickering anxiously. "Revooooolting sharp blaaaadey things."

"It's not for you," said Tom, looking hopefully at Erwin Hornheaver. "Could you go and see if the sword's still there?"

"Fine. I've already smashed in a few doors this evening and I don't mind smashing another," replied Hornheaver and disappeared outside.

Hetty Hyssop went over to the window and watched him stamping off down the muddy street.

"What a gloomy night," she muttered. "What a dark, gloomy night. I don't know what to hope for more: that the sword is gone or that our friend Hornheaver finds it. . . ."

Blood and a Sharp Blade

Erwin Hornheaver found the sword in the Cherrycorns' attic. It was stuck between an empty birdcage and two cardboard boxes of old photos. And it was longer than Hetty Hyssop's outstretched arm and so heavy that Tom could barely lift it. Erwin Hornheaver, however, swished it to and fro in the lobby of his inn as if it weighed no more than a handheld vacuum cleaner.

"Hornheaver, stop waving that thing around!" Hetty Hyssop exclaimed, taking it from his hand and leaning it against the wall. "Well," she continued, as Hugo, full of loathing, examined the cold, shimmering metal. "The mud is already seeping in through the downstairs windows, and if this demon is planning to return tonight, as Tom suspects, we've got one or two hours at the most. We all know that ghosts are particularly partial to the hour before dawn. That's why I'm going to make this brief." She cleared her throat, took a little can out of her bag, opened it, and held it out to Tom. "Here," she said. "Before I forget: Since you're crazy enough to go through with this, put three of these lozenges under your tongue and let them dissolve slowly. At least they'll give you back some energy." Then she turned to Erwin Hornheaver. "You've still got a choice, Erwin," she said. "You can still get into your car and drive to safety before the muddy final act begins. If your car hasn't sunk, that is."

"Out of the question," replied Erwin Hornheaver. "I'm not going to miss all the fun."

"Good." Hetty Hyssop nodded. "Then we're a foursome. That's not many of us, but it's not too few, either. Or would you prefer not to cross your ghostly colleague's path, Hugo?"

"Heeeee'll prooooobably rip us up in the air," breathed Hugo. "But soooo what? I've got leeeeeast of all to loooose. After all, I'm alreeeeeady dead."

"Well said," Hetty Hyssop agreed, suppressing a laugh. "OK, then. There's only one way to render a minotaurean demon harmless. Tom's already mentioned the account: Eugène de la Motette, chemist and demon-hunter, managed it in the sixteenth century and wrote down his experiences. The demon

he faced had, together with his followers, already killed the inhabitants of three villages. Motette made a circle of highly flammable material, and in the middle he put the only bait that a minotaurean demon can't resist. . . ."

"And what, may I ask, is that?" said Erwin Hornheaver hoarsely.

"A bucket full of blood," replied Hetty Hyssop.

Tom swallowed, and Erwin Hornheaver rubbed his stubbly chin. "The red finger paint we had the lad drink wouldn't do, would it?" he growled.

Tom held his hand to his stomach. "Finger paint?" he asked weakly.

"No, it definitely won't do," replied Hetty Hyssop. "But is there a doctor's office in the village that might have a blood supply?"

Erwin Hornheaver nodded. "I'm sure I'll be able to find something," he said. "Carry on. About this Mr. Quartet or whatever he was called."

"Motette, Eugène de la Motette. Yes." Hetty Hyssop rubbed the tip of her nose and glanced at her watch. The hands were still moving in the right direction. "Motette hid himself behind a wall, just a few feet away from the bait. And as soon as the demon began to devour the blood, Motette sprang out of his hidey-hole, set fire to the circle so that his opponent suddenly found himself surrounded by flames, with no way for his followers to rush to his aid, and" – Hetty Hyssop took a deep breath – "cut the demon in half right down the middle with a sword. Then he lost consciousness, as he put it. When Motette woke up

119

again, the demon had disappeared along with his entire band of followers. Only the gigantic horns were still lying in the mud. And they glowed for two whole days afterward, as if they had a light burning inside them. Since then, there have been no reports of these horned demons, which seem to be half bull, half human. Although Motette did suspect that there had to be a second specimen somewhere — one that had the head of a human and the body of a bull."

"Well, our demon has a bull's head, too," Tom said thoughtfully. "That contradicts his theory." He looked uneasily at the sword, which was still leaning against the door. "What if you don't slash him right down the middle?"

Hetty Hyssop merely shrugged. "I don't know."

Erwin Hornheaver stared at the sword, too. "Have you got any idea how such a monster comes into being?" he asked. "I mean, with ghosts there are normally stories about why they're haunting — because someone walled them up alive or because they're being punished for their evil deeds. . . ." He gave Hugo a suspicious look and stopped talking.

"What's that loooook suuuuupposed to mean?" breathed Hugo. "Eeeevil deeeeeds — what nonsense!"

Tom grinned. "Hugo fell off a roof when he was sleepwalking," he said. "The whole story is a bit embarrassing. Isn't that right, Hugo?"

Hugo merely turned his pale back on him, offended.

Hetty Hyssop explained, "People believe that minotaurean demons have a pretty horrible history. It's well known that, in earlier times, humans were afraid of disease and natural catastrophes, so they tried to get in their gods' good books by making sacrifices of all sorts of animals — sometimes humans as well. Many ghost experts believe that animal-human demons were the result of barbaric rituals such as these. The minotaurean demon is just one of these creepy creatures. Its thirst for blood fits with this explanation, as does its tendency to appear at ancient pagan shrines."

"Ghastly," murmured Erwin Hornheaver at the thought of such pagan rituals. "The things humans do when they're afraid."

"Yes, I sometimes think that fear is the root of all misery," said Hetty Hyssop, standing up with a sigh. "And I'm afraid we'll all be having more than enough fear tonight, but let's get on with it. You'll gather up the bait, will you, Hornheaver?"

Erwin Hornheaver nodded.

"One last question," he growled, already standing in the doorway. "Who's going to do the business with the sword?"

"I'll do it," replied Hetty Hyssop. "But I'd feel a whole lot better if you were waiting in the wings. I fear this is a night we just can't plan precisely. After all, we're dealing with the demon's followers as well. I just hope the circle of fire works as well for us as it did for our colleague Motette. But that's no more than a hope." She looked at her watch and froze.

"Oh my goodness!" she burst out. "My watch is going backward. We've barely got half an hour!"

The Zargoroth

The mud in front of the church was already so deep that Tom could barely make his way through it. The heavy brown mush sloshed around his knees whilst Hugo floated above it, not getting even the tiniest bit of his pale skin dirty. Panting, Tom stopped for a moment to catch his breath. The ground was heaving beneath his feet. The mud trembled ever more violently, as if a gigantic animal were stirring in the depths of the Earth. Tom shook his head anxiously. The vicarage had already sunk up to its windows in mud. Of several other houses, only the roofs were still visible.

"Yooooou'd better get a mooooove on!" cried Hugo, floating down onto the huge stone altar.

"Yeah, yeah!" growled Tom, pulling a large plastic container out of his backpack. Then he checked out the distance between himself and the altar and nodded, satisfied. "Yes, I think it'll fit," he muttered. "Now the stuff just has to stick to the mud. Wait a sec. . . . Hey, Hugo!" he hissed, waving to the ASG. "What about a nice sticky slimy trail?"

Grumbling, Hugo got up and put his pale feet in the mud. "That's revooooolting!" he breathed, leaving behind a glistening slimy trail with every step he took.

"Don't make such a fuss," whispered Tom. "You're not normally so squeamish." Then he opened the plastic container, reached inside, and scattered a coarse gray powder onto Hugo's trail. When the pair had finished, they were left with a large shimmering circle around the altar, barely visible in the darkness. "Well, that's that, I think," whispered Tom, straining his eyes to peer into the night.

The fog had lifted. Only the altar was still surrounded by some mist. "Definitely not a good sign!" muttered Tom.

"What?" asked Hugo.

"That the fog's gone," Tom replied in a whisper. "I bet that means showtime for the Prince of Demons!"

He looked around again, and this time he saw what he was looking for: Erwin Hornheaver and Hetty

Hyssop were striding across the muddy square, carrying a large cauldron between them.

"My goodness, I'll never set foot in mud or bogs again!" moaned Hetty Hyssop, helping Hornheaver lift the cauldron onto the altar. "My legs feel as if I've already walked twice around the world this evening."

"Is the cauldron full of . . . ?" Tom could barely bring himself to say the word.

"Blood?" Erwin Hornheaver shook his head. "No. Unfortunately we can only serve up a very thin blood soup to the demon. We found three pathetic bags of blood in the doctor's fridge; the rest is grape juice and ketchup. Now we just have to hope that this demon's sense of smell isn't too refined."

Tom looked anxiously at Hetty Hyssop. "And that's going to work?"

"I've added two sachets of **A**rtificial **B**lood **A**roma to the cauldron," Hetty Hyssop reassured him. "As you know, the powder's a standard component of our kit. After all, there are loads of ghosts who are attracted by the smell of blood. But let's get on with it."

She inspected the circle that Tom and Hugo had made. "Aha! You used Hugo's slime to secure the fire

circle. Excellent. Have we all got our equipment? Helmets, spark sprayers, protective goggles . . ."

The other three nodded. Erwin Hornheaver was wearing a builder's hard hat instead of a ghosthunter's protective helmet. It was, as Hetty Hyssop said, not ideal, but definitely better than no helmet at all.

"What about the sword?" Tom pushed his glasses straight and examined his spark sprayer for the second time. The contraption was similar to a water pistol and looked pretty harmless, but it spat out sparks like a bundle of fireworks. Ghosts hate these sparks: They bite their pale skin like fleas. A spark sprayer will keep a ghost at bay for a fair while, although not even an ASG would actually be scared off by one.

"I've got the sword," said Erwin Hornheaver, pulling the heavy object from under his jacket. He held it out to Hetty Hyssop with a broad grin. "Where do you want it, madam? You can obviously fit a fair few things in your bag, but this thing here . . ."

"Hand it over," said Hetty Hyssop, slipping the sword into her coat belt. Then she looked around, frowning. "I think we are best off hiding there," she said, pointing to three big blocks sticking up out of the mud behind the altar. "We've walked across everywhere else."

Tom nodded. "As soon as the circle's on fire, we all secure our section. I'm taking the left part, Hugo the right, and Erwin's in the middle."

"Can you box with ghosts?" asked Erwin Hornheaver.

"I wooouldn't recooommend it," breathed Hugo.

Hetty Hyssop climbed the steps to the altar. "Shall I wait for him under there?" she asked, peering under the big stone table.

"No way," replied Tom. "He'd rip your head off as soon as you came creeping out."

"Yes, he probably would," said Hetty Hyssop, standing up again. Deep in thought, she went back down the steps. As she put her foot on the bottommost step, the stone underneath trembled so violently that she almost fell head over heels. Tom and Erwin Hornheaver likewise had great difficulty staying upright. The entire church square heaved as if the whole Earth were opening up beneath the mud. Tom quickly pulled his GES out of his pocket.

"Here we go!" he cried. The mud parted sluggishly, like slow-moving lava, and a crater opened up in the middle of the church square.

"Hide, Tom, hide!" yelled Hetty Hyssop, rushing toward the stone blocks. Hugo and Erwin Hornheaver had already disappeared behind them.

"But the circle!" cried Tom, looking anxiously over at the glistening trail. The mud still hadn't swallowed it up.

"Come on!" yelled Hetty Hyssop. "Run for it!" And Tom ran for it. Or, rather, he tried to, but he could hardly move. The mud sucked at his boots as if the ground itself wanted to throw him to the Prince of Demons.

"Heeee's cooooooming!" he could hear Hugo howling. "Heeeeee's coooomiiiiing!"

Tom tugged desperately at his boots until the mud finally let them go with a *squelch*! Trembling and with his mouth as dry as a bone, he reached one of the blocks and pressed himself against the protective stone.

Just in time. Dripping figures floated out of the muddy crater. Moaning and howling, they rose up in the air, flew like trails of mist around the church steeple, then sank down again. They were waiting for the arrival of their master. What they didn't realize was that four others were waiting for him, too: three living, breathing, warm-blooded humans and one icy cold ASG.

A terrible silence fell across the deserted village. A deep, wild snorting sound boomed from the crater. And then they saw the Zargoroth.

His horny head appeared from the mud, his eyes glowing as if they were about to burn holes in the dark cloak of night. Sulfurous yellow steam poured from his nostrils, and as his shaggy upper body emerged from the mud he emitted such a hideous bellow that Tom had to press his hands to his ears. During his ghosthunting career he had witnessed many terrible sights, but nothing had ever made such an icy shiver run down his spine as the sight of this mud-dripping, bull-headed demon.

For a moment he closed his eyes and tried to breathe slowly. He couldn't begin to imagine how, with his knees trembling like this, he was supposed to get to the circle and set fire to it. But this vague feeling of panic was as much part and parcel of ghosthunting as were twitching eyebrows and a dry mouth. You just had to ignore it.

When Tom opened his eyes again, the Zargoroth was standing at full height in the Bogpool church square. He seemed much bigger to Tom than he'd been in the cave, but maybe he was mistaken there, too. He could hear the monster snorting as his burning eyes stared into the night. The crater that had spat out the Prince of Demons and his followers closed up behind them, squelching and slurping, and the Zargoroth raised his hideous head and sniffed the air. Tom pressed himself up against the stone, hardly daring to breathe.

Erwin Hornheaver, who was hiding behind the second slab, had clenched his gigantic fists and was staring at the demon with wide-open eyes. They all knew: If the demon spotted one of them, their entire plan would be destroyed.

"If he sees us now . . ." Tom preferred not to take that thought any further.

Hetty Hyssop herself was evidently anxious. Tom noticed the way her hand was closed around the sword. She had made up an extra-strong potion of the scented water that would cover up their human scent, but what did she know about a demon's sense of smell?

The Zargoroth still stood as if rooted to the spot, legs apart, head raised, as his followers floated above him, whispering and sighing. Then he took a step forward. And then another. He strode toward the altar. Tom breathed a sigh of relief. The Zargoroth had scented the blood.

Grunting, he sprang up the stone steps, licked his lips, bared his pale teeth — and plunged his head into the huge cauldron.

Silently, Hetty Hyssop pushed her way out from behind one of the stone blocks and crept behind the back of the demon.

Tom, however, ran toward the circle, already holding his lighter. The circle shone as it moved over the mud. His feet got stuck again, and he saw to his horror that the Zargoroth's ghostly followers were floating toward the altar. Erwin Hornheaver couldn't help him, either: He was fighting the mud just as much as Tom was.

"Hugo!" cried Tom in despair, sinking back down yet again. "Hugo, set fire to the circle!"

The next moment, Hugo's icy fingers grabbed the lighter from his hand. Tom saw the Zargoroth pull his head out of the cauldron with a jerk. But the demon had noticed the danger behind him too late.

Grinning maliciously, Hugo set fire to the protective circle — just as the ghosts were about to hurry to their master's aid, howling and screeching. The fire blazed high up into the black sky, the flames reaching for them with hot tongues. Horrified, they retreated — and their prince was left standing alone in front of the stone altar.

He looked even more hideous with a ketchup-stained mouth.

Threateningly he lowered his head, snorted, and stared all around him. Then he grunted, baffled, and spread his clawed hands. Hetty Hyssop stood at the bottom of the steps, looking up at him.

"This place doesn't belong to you, Zargoroth!" she cried, pulling the sword from her belt. "Let's call it quits, and don't ever let us see you again among humans. Or it will be your doom."

Panting and baring its teeth, a Ghost Dog sprang through the ring of fire to where Tom was standing. Tom drove it back with his spark sprayer and threw a tennis ball into its mouth, which was wide open with anger. (Gentle reader: These little balls are very effective with Ghost Dogs. It takes them hours to force them out of their throats.) Then Tom looked around wildly. He could hear the other ghosts screeching and howling, but none of them had followed the dog. The heat shield of the fire was holding them back. Only every now and then did a pale arm or a ghostly face poke through the flames. At the moment, Erwin Hornheaver was whacking the stinking fingers of a STKNOG, and Hugo was visibly enjoying giving one of the smaller BOSGs a pinch on its impudent nose.

Hetty Hyssop, however, was still standing before the Zargoroth, her sword drawn.

The demon stared at the dully gleaming blade, raised his horns, and pointed one of his clawed hands at her.

"Baaaaaaduuuuuu!" the demon howled.

There was a deathly silence. Only the flames crackled behind Tom. He knew he needed to keep an eye on the circle, but he simply couldn't take his eyes off the angry minotaur. Erwin Hornheaver seemed to react the same way. Even Hugo had forgotten the ghosts behind him. They hadn't uttered a sound since their master had spoken.

The Zargoroth took a stiff-legged step toward Hetty Hyssop. He was now just two steps above her, towering over her and examining her mockingly with his glowing eyes.

Tom stuffed the interpreter into his ear. He could translate *Badu* for himself. Every ghosthunter knew that it was an extremely contemptuous description for living people. You could translate it as something along the lines of "pig swill."

The Zargoroth took another step.

Hetty Hyssop didn't move a muscle. Tom found this quite astonishing, given how truly hideous the demon looked now. He seemed to be lit up from the inside; every one of his claws shimmered like a sharp little knife.

"*Mar to wiiiiraaaa, baduuu!*" he growled in a voice that sounded as if it were booming up from the

135

gloomiest of all graves. "You're going to be my slave, pig swill!"

Hetty Hyssop stood her ground. She still didn't move a muscle. Her hand merely tightened its grip slightly on the handle of the sword. "Oh yes?" she said, her voice threateningly calm. "I think I see things a bit differently, thank you very much."

At that moment, something shot past Tom. He whirled around in terror, almost falling flat on his face in the mud, which was deeper than ever. Not one but *two* Ghost Dogs had leaped through the flames – and before Tom could aim the spark sprayer at them, they were already hanging on to Hetty Hyssop's arm, snarling. Naturally, their pale teeth didn't cause any damage – after all, they were just Danger Category Two ghosts – but they were stopping Hetty Hyssop from raising the sword. And the Zargoroth knew that full well.

He jumped down the last couple of steps and stood before her, snorting. Then he threw back his head triumphantly, bellowed with anticipation, and bared his hideous teeth. Hetty Hyssop was still desperately trying to shake off the Ghost Dogs.

"Hugo! Hornheaver! Help!" yelled Tom, leaping to her side and spraying so many sparks onto the dogs' pale fur that they jumped away, howling.

"Out of the way, Tom!" cried Hetty Hyssop, trying to raise the sword — but her arms lacked strength after being attacked by the dogs, and the heavy sword slipped out of her fingers and fell in the mud.

With one bound, the demon leaped between her and Tom, grabbed them both by the scruff of their necks, and held them aloft like captured rabbits. Tom could feel the Zargoroth's hot, stinking breath and the incredible strength of his clawed hands. They seemed to suck all courage and all hope from Tom's bones. He felt like a rag doll waiting to be torn to shreds by those black claws. *I've botched it!* he thought in despair, the demon's stink starting to make him feel faint. *Curses! How could I have turned my back on the ring of fire?*

He saw the flames dying down and more and more ghosts floating through the protective circle. *Where's Hugo?* he thought, aiming a kick at the Zargoroth's hideous bull's head — then he saw Erwin Hornheaver stomping toward the demon with a look of deadly loathing.

What's he up to? wondered Tom. But Hornheaver was already bending down, and when he stood up again he was holding the mud-spattered sword.

"Let them go at once, you horned monster!" he bellowed, waving the sword around so wildly that Tom feared for his arms and legs. The Zargoroth growled – shaking his prisoners so violently that Tom's teeth chattered – and laughed.

It was a truly horrible laugh.

"Oh, you find it funny, do you?" bellowed Erwin Hornheaver, prancing around the demon as if they were in a boxing ring. "Watch it, or I'll turn you into demon goulash! I'll cut you up into such tiny pieces that it'll take your ghost friends years to pick them all up!"

"Tom!" yelled Hetty Hyssop, and Tom saw she'd managed to extract her spark sprayer from her belt. "Aim at his side!" Then she started firing.

With a cry of rage, the demon dropped her in the mud. Tom tried to copy her, but his spark sprayer could manage only a thin trickle. The Zargoroth bellowed angrily, held him high in the air, and opened his terrible mouth directly underneath Tom's feet.

Well, my Ghosthunting Diploma's a lost cause now!

thought Tom, and was just about to shut his eyes so that he didn't have to see the terrible demon's teeth as they devoured him, when he saw Erwin Hornheaver raising his arm again. In it was the gigantic sword that had spent centuries peacefully drowsing in a cornfield.

"Legs up, Tom!" he bellowed – and struck the Zargoroth straight down the middle.

Such a moan coursed through the deserted village that the roof tiles flapped. The branches were torn off the bare trees, and the demon's entire band of ghostly followers was blown away by their mighty master's last powerful sigh.

Tom, however, could feel icy ASG fingers gently catching hold of him as the claws of the doomed demon were loosening their grip. Then a second abyssal moan blew him and Hugo away, over the village rooftops, over an empty field, until they finally landed with a bump on the damp ground.

"Ohmygoodnessohmygoodness!" groaned Tom, struggling to stand up. "Ohmygoodnessohmygoodness ohmygoodness!" He simply couldn't think of anything more intelligent to say. He could still picture the Zargoroth's teeth beneath the soles of his shoes, and smell his hot, stinking breath. Exhausted, he took off his misted-up glasses. "Are you OK, Hugo?" he asked. "What happened to the beast? All I saw was the sword."

"Dissooooooooooolved!" replied Hugo, unraveling a knot in his pale arm. "Dissooooolved into the air, nothing but stinking aaaaair left!"

"Hmm." Tom nodded, replaced his glasses, and looked around. There were still one or two pale figures dotted about the sky. "His followers seem to be leaving, too," he murmured. "I reckon the haunting of Bogpool is over for the time being. Now it's a question of what's happened to the mud. That can't exactly have dissolved into thin air."

But as Tom floated back to the village on Hugo's back, he saw that the mud did indeed seem to have dissolved into thin air. The ground beneath Tom's mud-splattered boots was as dry as a bone when the ASG set him back down in Bogpool's church square. It was almost as if a desert wind had swept through the village.

"Oh, there you are!" cried Hetty Hyssop when she spotted the pair. "We had no idea where to start looking for you."

"Where's the mud gone?" asked Tom, looking around. The altar was still standing there, and the stone slabs were still looming up from the ground. The air smelled of fire and scorched earth.

"Well, that was one almighty sigh the Zargoroth let out," said Hetty Hyssop. "It was like a giant hair dryer. The mud went dry and crumbly within seconds."

"What should I do with these?" asked Erwin

Hornheaver, approaching them with a massive pair of horns in his hands. "Our demonic friend left them behind before he vanished."

Tom fished his GES out of his pocket and passed it across the horns. "Clearly harmless," he announced, putting the sensor away again. "You know what?" he said to Erwin Hornheaver. "You've got a natural talent for ghosthunting. We'd have looked pretty sorry this past night without your help."

"I fear we wouldn't have looked like anything at all," said Hetty Hyssop, giving Hornheaver a grateful thump on the shoulders. "Tom's absolutely right. You'd make a top-class ghosthunter. Be warned, my friend: If we ever need that kind of energetic help again, I'll give you a call."

Erwin Hornheaver smiled and rubbed his large chin, embarrassed. "You do that!" he growled. "Bogpool can be a bit of a boring spot sometimes. And now that the ghosts have gone, it certainly isn't going to become any more exciting."

"How about meeee dropping in every nooooow and then?" Hugo generously suggested. "I could dooooo a bit of hooooowling on the church steeple or make the vicarage all sliiiimy. . . ."

"That's very kind, but I think everyone else will be glad there's been an end to all the haunting," said Erwin Hornheaver. "Thanks all the same, though; it's a nice thought, really it is."

Side by side, they strolled across the church square toward the Final Round. Hugo floated in front. Tom, though, kept stopping to look back at the stone altar, which still loomed up, gray and alien, in the middle of the square.

"So is there really a second one?" he murmured.

"A second one?" asked Erwin Hornheaver.

"Tom's thinking of the theory that there are always two specimens of Zargoroth," replied Hetty Hyssop.

"Oh yes, I remember!" growled Erwin Hornheaver. Thoughtfully, he swung the demon's horns. He was carrying them in one hand as if they weighed no more than a bird's egg. "Well, I prefer to think of it this way," he said as they arrived at the inn. "If this demon really was created by a bull sacrifice and a human sacrifice, then things were joined together that don't go together. And we've put it to rights again. Everything's as it should be, and the two now have their peace."

Hetty Hyssop smiled. "Interesting idea," she said, opening the door to the inn. "Yes, I like that idea. But

I have to contradict you all the same. There's no way everything's back to rights yet. Tom and I still have a score to settle. Haven't we, Tom?"

"Too right," replied Tom, trying to imagine the look on Lotan Slimeblott's face when he came marching into his office as fit as a fiddle.

Revenge Tastes Sweet

Professor Slimeblott turned as yellow as an old newspaper when Tom appeared, unannounced, in his office. "Tom!" he exclaimed. "Where have *you* been?"

"You know full well where he's been," replied Hetty Hyssop, barging through the door behind Tom. "Good evening, Lotan."

Slimeblott turned the color of a very ripe lemon. "H – Hetty!" he stammered. "I don't understand –"

"How we're still alive and standing in front of you?" Tom finished his sentence. "Well, it's certainly no thanks to you. Is it, Hugo?"

"Noooo, it certainly iiiisn't!" breathed Hugo, floating elegantly through Professor Slimeblott's mahogany door.

"You dare to bring that ASG here?" cried Lotan Slimeblott, rising from his chair. His voice almost cracked.

"Hugo," said Hetty Hyssop without taking her eyes off the professor. "Shut the door and give me the key."

"With the greatest oooof pleeeeasure!" breathed Hugo, throwing her the key. Hetty Hyssop caught it in one hand and slipped it into her pocket.

His fingers trembling, Lotan Slimeblott reached for the coffee mug standing on his desk and took a big sip. Tom glanced quickly at Hetty Hyssop.

"Hugo," he said. "Just wobble over there and have a sniff at the mug."

Professor Slimeblott froze in horror as the ASG floated across to his desk with an evil smile and took the mug from his hand.

"Saltwaaaater!" reported Hugo, putting the mug back down on the desk in disgust. Lotan Slimeblott stared at him, full of hatred, and clung to his armchair.

"Don't you come near me, you revolting icy-fingered thing!" he growled. "You disgusting slime-spilling nobody of a ghost!"

"Very interesting!" said Hetty Hyssop, folding her arms across her chest. "Isn't it, Tom?"

"Absolutely," said Tom. "Slurpers always did have a strong aversion to ASGs."

"What . . . what's that supposed to mean?" Professor Slimeblott burst out, taking another sip from his mug. "What kind of nonsense are you talking, Tom? And what happened to the assignment I gave you?"

"Oh yes, the assignment . . . umm, that's a bit of a complicated story." Tom came up to the desk. "Hugo, bring over the professor's present!" he said.

Hugo disappeared through the door and returned with the Zargoroth's horns. He dropped them on Professor Slimeblott's desk with a bump.

"You know, I guess my diploma's down the drain," Tom continued as the professor stared, dumbfounded, at the horns. "I did catch the unknown ghost, but I let it go again so I could get a different ghost. I'm sure you know what I'm talking about, don't you?"

Professor Slimeblott made no reply. He downed what was left of his saltwater, wiped his lips with the back of his trembling hand — and floated up to the ceiling.

"That's impossible!" he cried, flapping his arms and legs like someone learning to swim. "Nobody can finish off a Zargoroth, especially not a little squirt like you!"

Tom stepped aside just in time as the professor spat at him.

"'Little squirt'? Well, that really isn't very kind!" he said.

"My dear Lotan!" Hetty Hyssop called up to Slimeblott. "At first I thought you'd assigned Tom this test out of sheer spite and envy. After all, you always were an extremely unpleasant character. I assumed you wanted to get your revenge on me in this brutal way, and that you were jealous of Tom's fantastic success, what with him being so much younger than you. But then I thought again. . . ."

"Hugo, watch it!" yelled Tom, for Lotan Slimeblott was making for one of the windows. Hugo cut off his route, poking his cold fingers into his chest so that the professor started to spin. With the greatest difficulty he paddled up to the lamp that dangled from the ceiling, then held on tightly to the cable.

"Oh, just stop all these pathetic attempts to escape!" said Hetty Hyssop impatiently. "You know that it's very hard for even fully grown Slurpers to do anything against ASGs. Not to mention amateurs like you."

Lotan Slimeblott spat again, but this time it only hit his desktop.

"Well, then, as we said, we thought it was just your character at first!" said Tom, running his finger over the Zargoroth's horns. "But then we had another idea: Humans who are attacked by Slurpers have to take pepper pills for two months afterward, or else they gradually turn into Slurpers themselves — into pretty harmless sub-Slurpers, in fact, whose main characteristics are malice and a pronounced lust for revenge — along with an insatiable thirst for saltwater."

"Admit it, Lotan!" said Hetty Hyssop, pulling from her large bag something that looked like a spray gun. "You didn't take the pepper pills I gave you at the time."

"Put that **G**host-**S**ucker-**U**pper away!" bellowed Lotan Slimeblott. "Pepper pills, pah! Surely you don't think that I believe in any of your potions and pastes! You wanted to poison me! Yes, you did! I wish that Zargoroth had spiked you and your ridiculous assistants on his horns like kebabs! I wish he'd ripped you to shreds in the air and turned you into confetti!"

"Yes, yes, as I said, you always were a more than unsavory character!" continued Hetty Hyssop, screwing a large plastic container onto the Ghost-Sucker-Upper.

Lotan Slimeblott's face was shimmering a luminous yellow, rather like a neon sign. He took a nosedive and tried to grab one of the bottles next to his desk lamp, but Tom got there first.

"A bit more saltwater?" he asked, shaking his head as he put the bottle into his backpack. "No, that's the worst thing you could possibly do. The state you're in, it'll take at least a year for you to be despookified. And it won't be pleasant – I can tell you that much."

Professor Slimeblott gave a howl and tried once again to escape through one of the windows, but Hugo had been paying attention. Howling and spitting, Lotan Slimeblott retreated from his icy ASG fingers.

"Tom, you take over!" said Hetty Hyssop, handing him the sucker-upper. "After all, you're the one he set his devious trap for."

Tom checked one final time that the plastic container was properly attached – and took aim. Lotan Slimeblott tried to squeeze himself behind a cupboard, but Tom opened the valve on the sucker-upper before the professor could hide. They heard a sharp hissing sound, and Lotan Slimeblott's figure became longer and longer, before fluttering like a piece of paper in a gale-force wind. And then it disappeared with a screech into the nozzle of the sucker-upper.

"Well, how about that," said Tom, peering into the plastic container. Professor Slimeblott was crouching inside it, looking flabbergasted – and still a bit stretched, despite having been shrunk to the size of a guinea pig.

"Ha-ha-ha, yoooou miserable Sluuuuuurper, pah!" said Hugo, floating over to Tom.

"Oh, he still wasn't a real Slurper, or he'd have given us more trouble than that!" said Tom. He unscrewed the plastic container from the sucker-upper, quickly shut it off with a special air-permeable lid, and gave it to Hetty Hyssop. "Here you are. I believe this is a case for the **CDEGH**." (That is, gentle readers, the **C**linic for the **DE**spookification of **G**host**H**unters.)

"I think so, too," said Hetty Hyssop, stuffing Lotan Slimeblott into her capacious handbag.

"But what's going to happen with my diploma?" Tom asked helplessly as they made their way out of Slimeblott's office. "Presumably I'll have to get some-one to assign me another field test, won't I?"

"Nonsense!" Hetty Hyssop put her arm around his shoulders. "Erwin Hornheaver and I already gave the examinations board a detailed account of what you did in Bogpool, whereupon they unanimously voted to award you the FIGHD on the spot and with no further conditions."

"The FIGHD?" Tom gasped. He looked at Hetty Hyssop disbelievingly. "The **FI**fth **G**host**H**unting **D**iploma! But – but – but only fourteen people in the world have got that, as far as I know. Including you."

Hetty Hyssop smiled. "Well, now it's fifteen," she said. "And you're the youngest of them by a long shot, Tom, champion ghosthunter."

"Congraaaaatulaaaaations!" breathed Hugo, lifting Tom up on his shoulders.

"Hugo, put me down at once!" cried Tom.

But Hugo was having none of it.

In Case of
an Encounter

Ravenous readers, as told in the pages you have just devoured as greedily as the Zargoroth did that fateful bucket of ketchup, Tom indeed battled to the death with a bull-headed demon in *Ghosthunters and the Muddy Monster of Doom!*, but he also had to face an even scarier foe:

The unfair teacher.

These evil beasts lurk in the hallways of almost every institute of higher learning – no doubt your own educational experience has already confirmed this.

So if the school principal appears as pale as skim milk, or the Spanish instructor has a strange, insatiable thirst for saltwater, be warned! Your report card may be at the mercy of a Slurper.

Confronted with the same bone-chilling conundrum – prehistoric minotaur demon or modern-day mean teacher – which would you, fledgling ghosthunter, choose?

In the statistically impossible and yet hey-you-never-know event of meeting both monstrosities — whether in the muddy square of a medieval village or the musty stacks of the public library — all ghosthunters committed to their continued existence are strongly recommended to consume a few pages more. . . .

PRECAUTIONARY MEASURES
Against Ghosts in General

- The color red — as in socks, sweaters, curtains, sofas, and so on. If you ever happen upon a so-called ghosthunter with walls in any other color, be on your guard.

- Raw eggs, for throwing.

- Food, for eating: Serious ghosthunters always carb-load before getting down to business; on a full stomach it's easier to withstand the sensation of a ghost floating through you.

- Salt: It burns.

- Mirrors: Hang them on your red-painted walls; wear pocket-sized varieties when in the field.

- A spare pair of shoes: Depending on the variety of ghost, it will leave a trail that's sticky, snowy, muddy, etc. If in the thrill of the chase your sneakers get glued in place, it helps to have a backup.

- Graveyard dirt that's been gathered at night (*see* Ghosthunters and the Incredibly Revolting Ghost! *for specifics*).

- Chapels and crypts: With the exception of a few species, ghosts wouldn't be caught dead in these places. Recommended as locations for regrouping when a ghosthunt goes wrong.

- Daylight: Aim to accomplish the bulk of your ghosthunting during the day, as hauntings tend to intensify in the dark.

- And no matter what, do not – do NOT – carry a flashlight on ghosthunting expeditions. The beam of a flashlight will drive a ghost into a violent rage.

- But don't bother whispering: Most ghosts can't hear very well, and rely instead on their sense of smell. (For this and reasons of basic human hygiene, ghosthunters should make a habit of bathing.)

IN CASE OF AN ENCOUNTER WITH A NEPGA
(NEgative Projection of a Ghostly Apparition)

• Buckle up your neutralizer belt: Beltless contact with a NEPGA causes fourteen days of muscle cramps, minimum.

• Be rude: Contrary to what you've been taught in charm school, decline to shake a NEPGA's hand. Doing so will you leave you stiff as a surfboard for a month — a highly impolite outcome, four out of five etiquette experts agree.

• Be ruder: Hurl invective to lure it into a trap. Proven categories of insult include comments about the ghost's papery appearance as well as universally offensive "Your momma . . ." jokes.

• Blast it with a mix of baking powder and scouring sand: The gritty coating will stop it from floating through walls and slow down its flying speed.

• But don't bother bonking it on the head with a hammer or a shovel or any other such implement, since it will only turn as limp as a licorice stick.

A POSTSCRIPT ABOUT PAWOGS
(PAle WObbly Ghosts)

• P.S. They're best combatted with laughing gas.

A TIDBIT ON THE TOPIC OF SCREECHERS

• The screech of the eponymous screecher is so
freakishly, shriekishly shrill, it has the power to bend
metal objects. This is useful if you happen to be
hunting ghosts with either a dented bike tire rim or a
twisted ice cream spoon: One screech and they'll
straighten out again. Otherwise, minus the aid of
Hyper-Sound Filters (HYSOFs), expect to be
rendered stone-deaf for up to thirteen days.

IF SUBJECTED TO A SLURPER ATTACK . . .

• Take pepper tablets for two months afterward. Side
effects to pepper pill-popping include nonstop
sneezing, so common sense suggests you stockpile
tissues, too. (Nonstop sneezing is still better than
being turned into a substandard Slurper with an
insatiable thirst for saltwater.)

TO RE-CREATE THE GHOSID
(GHOst SImulation Disguise)

• Paint your face a moldy green (*see Hyssop & Co.'s range of "Ghostly Pallor" creams for dry, combination, and pimple-prone skin; available in matte for a dull, lifeless finish or moisturizing for a graveyard-dewy glow*).

• Put on a pair of moldy green overalls: To achieve the proper degree of moldiness, break them in by trapping TIBIGs in damp basements and/or castle dungeons. (*For step-by-step instructions, see* Ghosthunters and the Totally Moldy Baroness!)

• Stink of cellars: another reason to go TIBIG-hunting.

• Stick with your spectacles: Plenty of ghosts wear glasses in the great beyond; yours won't give you away.

A PROVISO APROPOS OF THIRTEENTH
MESSENGERS
(a.k.a. GHODEs or GHOsts of DEath)

• Strap on protective goggles: One look at a Thirteenth Messenger with the naked eye and within the hour you're ghost toast.

- The protective goggles themselves are only good for a five-minute glance, so . . . no staring.

- If you've made the almost certainly fatal mistake of gazing upon a **GHODE** without protective gear and you're not already dead:

  – Gather up: cooking oil; marsh clover; red food coloring; lamps with red lightbulbs; the most powerful vacuum cleaner known to humankind; and two fellow ghosthunters, one who preferably is a member of the wrestling team, the other whose favorite hobby just happens to be housecleaning.

  – Drink the oil-clover-food-coloring concoction. It will, of course, taste repulsive.

  – Gaze into the burning red bulbs to banish flashing yellow lights from your sight.

  – Have the wrestler squeeze you till poisonous vapors stream out of your ears while the neat freak sucks up the deadly smoke with the vaccum cleaner.

IN CASE OF AN ENCOUNTER WITH A MINOTAUR DEMON
... you're probably already a goner, but ...

- Be on guard if clocks start turning backward.

- To bait a Zargoroth, set out a bucket of blood. Blood not sold by the bucketful in your neighborhood supermarket? Sprinkle a few sachets of Artificial Blood Aroma (a standard component of the ghosthunters' kit) into a fake-out potion of grape juice and ketchup.

- To corner a Zargoroth, surround it with a ring of fire. (It burns, burns, burns, the ring of fire.)

- To defeat a Zargoroth, slice it clean in half with a sword. Once halved, the beast will dissolve into thin air with a supersonically stinky howl.

- If you've already forgotten everything you just read, no worries: With the exception of Tom, Hetty, Hugo, Hornheaver, and Eugène de la Motette, no one has ever encountered this demon without losing his or her life or sanity. Best of luck, see you at the insane asylum.

Indispensable Alphabetical
APPENDIX OF ASSORTED GHOSTS

AG	**A**ncient **G**host
ASG	**A**veragely **S**pooky **G**host
BLAGDO	**BLA**ck **G**host **DO**g
BOSG	**BO**g and **S**wamp **G**host
CAG	**CA**stle **G**host
CG	**C**ellar **G**host
COHAG	**CO**mpletely **HA**rmless **G**host
FG	**F**ire **G**host
FOFIFO	**FO**ggy **FI**gure **FO**rmer
FOFUG	**FO**ggy **FU**g-**G**host
GG	**G**raveyard **G**host
GHADAP	**GH**ost with **A DA**rk **P**ast
GHODE	**GH**ost **O**f **DE**ath
GIHUFO	**G**host **I**n **HU**man **FO**rm
GILIG	**G**ruesome **I**nvincible **LI**ghtning **G**host
HIGA	**HI**storical **G**hostly **A**pparition
IRG	**I**ncredibly **R**evolting **G**host

MG	**M**arsh **G**host
MUWAG	**MU**ddy **WA**ters **G**host
NAG	**NA**ture **G**host
NEPGA	**NE**gative **P**rojection of a **G**hostly **A**pparition
PAWOG	**PA**le **WO**bbly **G**host
RR	**R**attle**R**
SLUG	**SLU**rper **G**host
STKNOG	**ST**inking **KNO**cking **G**host
SWG	**SW**ig **G**host
TIBIG	**TI**ny **BI**ting **G**host
TOHAG	**TO**tally **HA**rmless **G**host
TOMOB	**TO**tally **MO**ldy **B**aroness
WG	**W**ater **G**host
WHIWHI	**WHI**rlwind **WHI**rler
WL	**W**hite **L**ady

Miscellaneous Listing of
NECESSITOUS EQUIPMENT AND
NOTEWORTHY ORGANIZATIONS

ABA	**A**rtificial **B**lood **A**roma
ACH	**A**ir **CH**arger
CDEGH	**C**linic for the **DE**spookification of **G**host**H**unters
CECOCOG	**CE**ntral **CO**mmission for **CO**mbating **G**hosts
COCOT	**CO**ntact-**CO**mpression Trap
FIGHD	**FI**fth **G**host**H**unting **D**iploma
GEAS	**G**hostly **E**nergy **A**nti-**S**ensor
GES	**G**hostly **E**nergy **S**ensor
GHAS	**G**host**H**unting **AS**sociation
GHASEB	**G**host**H**unting **AS**sociation's **E**xamining **B**oard
GHUGL	**GH**ost**HU**nting **G**uide**L**ines
GHOM	**GHO**st **M**agnetizer
GHOSID	**GHO**st-**SI**mulation **D**isguise
GSI	**G**host-**S**peak **I**nterpreter

GSU	Ghost-Sucker-Upper
HID	Heat-Intensifying Device
HYSOF	HYper-SOund Filter
LOAG	List Of All Known Ghosts
NENEB	NEgative-NEutralizer Belt
OFFCOCAG	OFFice for COmbating CAstle Ghosts
RCFCAG	Retention Center For Criminally Aggressive Ghosts
RICOG	Research Institute for COmbating Ghosts
ROGA	Register Office for Ghostly Apparitions
SEV	Spook Energy Visualizer
SGHD	Second GhostHunting Diploma
SPSP	SPark SPrayer
THGHD	THird GhostHunting Diploma

Unleash the secrets within...

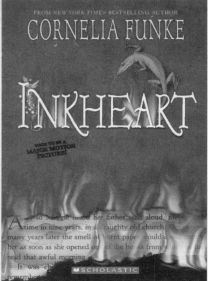

Meggie and her father Mo share a peaceful life together. But one evening a mysterious stranger forces Mo to reveal his extraordinary gift—a gift Meggie may also possess. Discover their remarkable secret—and how it changes their lives forever—in this thrilling adventure.